The XYZs of Being Wicked

The XYZs of Being Wicked

Lara Chapman

ALADDIN M!X
NEW YORK   LONDON   TORONTO   SYDNEY   NEW DELHI

ALADDIN M!X
Simon & Schuster Children's Publishing Division
1230 Avenue of the Americas, New York, NY 10020
First Aladdin M!X edition July 2014
Text copyright © 2014 by Lara Chapman
Cover illustration copyright © 2014 by Coco Masuda
All rights reserved, including the right of reproduction in whole or in part in any form.
ALADDIN is a trademark of Simon & Schuster, Inc., and related logo is a
registered trademark of Simon & Schuster, Inc.
ALADDIN M!X and related logo are registered trademarks of Simon & Schuster, Inc.
Also available in an Aladdin hardcover edition.
For information about special discounts for bulk purchases, please contact
Simon & Schuster Special Sales at 1-866-506-1949 or business@simonandschuster.com.
The Simon & Schuster Speakers Bureau can bring authors to your live event. For more
information or to book an event, contact the Simon & Schuster Speakers Bureau
at 1-866-248-3049 or visit our website at www.simonspeakers.com.
Book designed by Jeanine Henderson
The text of this book was set in Fairfield.
Manufactured in the United States of America 0614 OFF
10 9 8 7 6 5 4 3 2 1
Library of Congress Control Number 2014938969
ISBN 978-1-4814-0108-1 (hc)
ISBN 978-1-4814-0107-4 (pbk)
ISBN 978-1-4814-0109-8 (eBook)

For my sisters, who inspire me every day with their strength, wit, and compassion

Acknowledgments

No book makes it to the shelves without an entire cast of behind-the-scenes characters!

I must begin with my agent, Holly Root. You have blessed my life with your intelligence, wit, and razor-sharp business sense. Without you, I'd still be entering contests and praying for a break! Thank you for always believing in me.

A huge thanks to my editor at Aladdin, Alyson Heller, for falling in love with Hallie and the gang. You made *XYZs* the amazing book that it is and me a better writer. A million thanks wouldn't be enough!

My precious kids, Caleb and Laney . . . you are the reason I was put on this crazy planet. Thank you for making every day worth living and for loving me, faults and all!

Bill, someone once called me a wordsmith, which is ironic because I can't think of a proper way to thank you here. You restored my faith in love and in myself. I will spend forever loving you every bit as much as you love me.

To my parents . . . neither of you ever held one of my

books, but don't think for a minute I didn't hear you in my head when I was stuck on a scene or doubting my writing ability. I love you and miss you more every single day.

Whoa! I can't forget a shout-out to my Suh-weet Success Sisters—Alex Ratcliff, Kimberle Swaak, Diane Wied, Koreen Gonzales, and the crazy-talented Margie Lawson. Thank you for critiquing honestly and cheering endlessly, both on and off the mountain. I seriously couldn't have written this book without you.

And finally, to my readers . . . thank you for picking up this book and spending some time with Hallie. I hope she taught you to believe in yourself, work hard, and stay focused. And don't forget to laugh a lot along the way. Life's short—live without regrets!

The XYZs of Being Wicked

Dowling Academy

P.O. Box 12

Cobb, Texas 78601

Dear Miss Hallie Simon,

It's my honor to welcome you to the Dowling Academy School of Witchcraft. Dowling admits young girls like yourself based exclusively on your Wiccan lineage.

You are certain to have many questions, some of which will be answered when you move in on September 2nd. Please plan to arrive promptly between 3:00 p.m. and 4:00 p.m. You will be signed in, shown to your dorm, and introduced to your roommate and dorm mother. Please note the following strict packing guidelines.

• Pack all belongings in your family trunk and the enclosed duffel bag. No additional luggage will be permitted.

• For your arrival please wear blue jeans and the enclosed red polo with the Dowling Academy insignia. White tennis shoes are required. Your school uniform will be provided upon your arrival.

• Seekers are not allowed access to Internet technology, including cell phones. Please do not bring one with you.

• MP3 players are permitted if used responsibly.

• Cosmetics should not be packed. That privilege is not given to Seekers.

• Bedding will be provided.

• Decorating your room is permitted, within reason.

On behalf of our prestigious staff, current students, and extended family of supporters, I welcome you to the Dowling Academy sisterhood. Your legacy awaits you.

Regards,
Headmistress Veronica Fallon

P.S. As a direct descendent of Dowling's finest hedge witch, your great-great-grandmother, Elsa Whittier Simon, it is your karama, your life's purpose, to follow in her extraordinary foot-steps. As a hedge witch, your ability to be a healer and your deep love and understanding of nature make you a critical link in the Dowling Coven. Your attendance at Dowling will ensure the survival of your family's Wiccan heritage.

One

Mom's voice is clipped and irritated when she taps her watch. "Tick tock, Hallie."

I keep my eyes on the television. "When this is over."

The television clicks off, and I huff out a big breath. I hate it when she does that.

"I'm not packing for you, no matter how long you put it off."

I lie down on the couch and groan. "I'll do it later. Who knows when I'll get to see my shows again."

"One, two . . ."

"Really? You're counting? I'm eleven, Mom. Not five."

She grabs my legs and drops them to the floor. "Now."

Moving more slowly than honey in a snowstorm, I drag myself to the attic door.

I hate attics. And basements. They're the soulless pits of a house, and I have no use for either one of them. Except today. Today, I *have* to climb into the attic. It doesn't matter that the last time I was in the attic, I fell and landed face-first in the biggest spiderweb any spider has ever created in the history of the world.

I'm on my third jump to reach the cord hanging from the attic door when Dad appears. He drops a step ladder in front of me. "The definition of 'insanity' is doing the same thing and—"

"Expecting different results," I finish. Dad's a total quote junkie. This particular Einstein quote has been repeated in my house so many times, I have it memorized.

I take two steps on the small ladder, grab the cord, and pull it down.

"Packing? Already?" he teases, knowing Mom's been nagging me for a week to pack.

"Funny, Dad." I give him a smile, and my heart pinches. I'm going to miss him. I'm going to miss Mom. I'm going to miss my dog, Charlie. The only thing I won't miss is the heartless Kendall Scott, who has made it her personal mission in life to ensure I never rise above the level of social scum at school.

Dad rubs his hands together like he's warming them over a fire. "Exciting stuff, Hallie."

A flame of panic spreads through my stomach. I douse it with the reminder that I'm starting over in a new school with new kids. Dowling's my do-over.

I look up the attic stairs, then back at him. He knows how I feel about attics. "Want me to turn the light on?" Without waiting for me to answer, he climbs the stairs, yanks the light cord, and comes back down. "It's all yours."

Watching Dad walk off, I wish I'd asked him to go up with me. I grab the handle of the folding stairs that lead to the attic and gently place my foot on the first step. It creaks lightly under my weight.

You're being ridiculous, Hallie Faith Simon. Climb the steps, clean out the trunk, pack, and be done with it.

I hold my breath and take the rest of the steps quickly, exhaling when I reach the top. The attic is as musty and menacing as I remember.

I scan the neatly stacked boxes, plastic tubs, and plywood walking paths. I place one foot on the wood to test its strength, then gingerly walk the plank. The trunk is exactly where Mom said it would be—under the window, covered in dust, daring me to open it.

I drop to my knees and blow on the top of the trunk. Even after I open the window, the dust hangs in the air and I have to wave my hands in front of me to see better. Putting my hand on the metal latch, I close my eyes, and quickly lift the lid. When nothing jumps out and kills me, I peek through one eye to examine the trunk. Seems safe enough, so I dare to open both eyes. Carved on the inside of the lid is something I can't read. I trace my fingers over the cursive letters and try to pronounce the words.

Delicias fuge ne frangaris crimine, verum
Coelica tu quaeras, ne male dipereas;
Respicias tua, non cujusvis quaerito gesta
Carpere, sed laudes, nec preme veridicos;
Judicio fore te praesentem conspice toto.

Anxiety swims through me. I may not be able to read it, but I know these words will be important in my new world. Engraved below that are words I can actually read.

SIMON FAMILY TRUNK
DOWLING ACADEMY SCHOOL OF
WITCHCRAFT, Est. 1521

More curious than afraid, I peer into the trunk. Part of me hopes there's a copy of *Witchcraft for Dummies* inside, but all I find are two weird things that look like they belong in a museum.

A small stick that looks like a miniature totem pole leans in the corner of the trunk. Again I blow the dust off and lean in for a closer look. But I can't see it the way I want and slowly slip my hand into the trunk. I grab the stick and pull it out quickly, like rattlers are threatening to strike. When lightning doesn't fry me, I let out the breath I've been holding. Call me crazy, but digging in a dead witch's trunk puts this girl on edge.

The stick is so light, I can barely feel it in my hands as I hold it up to the sunlight. Symbols I don't recognize are carved into the stick, and instead of totally creeping me out, it calms me. I can't explain it, but something like relief washes over me.

I put the stick back into the trunk, and, braver than I thought possible, I grab the only other item in the trunk. A book of yellowed pages with an *S* embossed in the center fills my hands. I wipe the black leather cover and let my finger trace the *S*. Is the *S* for "Simon"?

Gently I open the cover and read the inscription.

This Book of Shadows Belongs to Elsa Whittier Simon.

I grin at the small angry letters scribbled at the bottom.

HANDS OFF!

I don't make friends easily, but I think I would have liked my great-great-grandmother.

I reread the inscription. *Book of Shadows*. Another part of my new life I know nothing about. Thumbing through the pages filled with perfect cursive handwriting, I stop at a dog-eared page.

Hear us now, the words of the witches,
The secrets we hide in the night.
Our magic is sought,
Invoke our power,
In this hour,
On this night.

I whisper the words as I read them, over and over again.

"Hal?"

The sound of my mother's voice behind me stops my

heart for a full second. I whip my head around, but before I can tell her how badly she scared me, wind swirls inside the attic, first soft and refreshing. Then churning faster and faster and faster, like an angry tornado. Boxes, papers, and pieces of insulation hurl through the room so fiercely, I can barely hold my place on the floor. I clutch the Book of Shadows to my chest to keep from losing it.

I attempt to scream through the storm. "Mom!"

The trunk seems to be the only thing not flying through the room, so I grab it in a death grip.

There's no reply from Mom, and I've lost sight of her in the storm debris.

My glasses begin sliding from my face, and I drop the Book of Shadows to hold them in place.

In that instant the room stills.

My eyes dart through the room, taking in the attic, the attic that should be filled with trash but looks exactly as it did when I first climbed the stairs.

Hand still clamped on the trunk, I take a shaky breath. What in the world just happened? Did I imagine it?

When I finally lock eyes with Mom, her body is frozen in fear.

No. I did not imagine this. What just happened scared

her even more than it terrified me, and I remind myself that she's as new to this as I am.

"What— Did you— How . . ." She stutters over her words, trying to make sense of the bizarro scene. All the relief I felt just moments ago has evaporated, and in its place is sheer panic.

I can't do this.

I can't do this.

I can't be a witch.

But a voice thunders in my head. *I have to do this.*

I toss the book into the trunk and shut the lid before dragging the piece of luggage closer to Mom. I need to get out of here and immediately pretend none of it happened, pretend I didn't cause the storm, and pretend I'm not going to a school for witches.

"See?" I say. "Didn't I tell you? Nothing good happens in attics."

Two

Standing in the registration line at Dowling, I struggle to keep a sweaty grip on my side of the family trunk. Dad's holding the other side, shoulders back, chest out, pride spewing out of him like an erupting volcano.

I grow more anxious as each minute passes. I was flabbergasted when my parents told me about Dowling and why I had to go. How could I have been a witch my whole life and never known? Dad's explanation involving lineage and some great-great-grandmother I never met made little sense. But I knew he was telling the truth. And I knew I had to go, no matter how badly I wanted to stay in my safe, predictable world.

There's only one girl in front of us. Like me, she's

in jeans, a red polo, and white shoes. Like me, she's white-knuckling one end of her family trunk, pretending there's nowhere else she'd rather be.

Finished signing in, the family follows an older Dowling student down a wide hallway. I steel myself for the reality that my parents are about to walk me to my dorm. Then leave. For good.

I trudge up to the table and come face-to-face with a plump woman with a bright smile and curly hair so dry, it looks like it could catch fire at any moment. I make a mental note of the name on her ID badge. Agnes Armstrong.

I take her in. Mascara is caked in globs on her short, stumpy eyelashes, and the deep red lipstick smeared across her lips has smudged onto her teeth. It's kind of a mess but somehow seems right on her.

"Well, hello there!" she says. "What's your name, sugar?"

I pull my eyes from her red-stained choppers. "Hallie. Hallie Simon."

Her eyes brighten and she raises her hand in the air. I just stare at it, confused. Surely she isn't trying to high-five me.

"You're one of my girls!" she announces, bouncing in her seat.

Since I have no idea what it means to be one of her girls, I just smile.

She waves her hand closer to me. "Well, don't leave me hanging."

I tap my hand to hers, quick as I can. In my old school, public high-fiving is a one-way ticket to merciless mocking.

"What does it mean, exactly, when you say Hallie is one of your girls?" Mom puts her hand on my shoulder, pulling me closer.

Miss Armstrong slaps her hands to her chest. "Where are my manners! I just get so excited when I meet my girls for the first time." She focuses her attention on me. "I'm your dorm mother, sweetie. I'll be your mom away from home."

Mom's hand tightens on my shoulder.

"If you're sick," she says, "I'll be the one to give you that TLC. Although . . ." Her brows draw together like she's realizing something for the first time. "I can't recall the last time a student fell ill at Dowling. Hmm. Curious."

"Excellent to hear." Dad shoots his hand in front of him. I brace myself for his booming salesman voice. "Phil Simon."

I cringe, waiting for Miss Armstrong's reaction.

"Well, now, isn't that a nice howdy-do!" she says, pumping his hand firmly. "Agnes Armstrong," she answers, the tone of her voice mimicking Dad's. She shifts her focus back to me. "But you can call me Miss A. All the girls do."

Miss A passes Mom a business card. "Now, I don't want you to worry about a thing. You can reach me anytime, night or day. Just call that number, and whatever you do, don't forget the code. I can't talk to you unless you have the code, even if I recognize your voice." She shakes her head abruptly. "No exceptions."

"What's the code?" Panic makes Mom's voice a little louder, a little more forceful, than usual.

"It's printed in the bottom right-hand corner. See it?"

I lean closer and see the small series of letters and numbers that seem to squirm and shift on the paper. The harder I look at the numbers, the more they seem to morph, to change. An 8 turns into an *S* and a *T* turns into a 7.

"Yeah, I see it." Mom looks at me, her face a jumbled mess of worry, confusion, and run-for-your-life fear.

"Now, let's see here," Miss A says, dragging a stubby finger down a sheet of blank paper in front of her. I shift so I can get a better look at the paper, but no matter which direction I move, the paper remains blank. If it *is* blank, what in the world is she looking at?

"Nope! Your roommate hasn't arrived yet. But I'm sure she'll be here lickety-split."

She grabs a large white envelope from a box beside her chair. She slides her hand across the envelope, and my name appears in perfect, fancy handwriting.

Or was it already there? Maybe I need new glasses.

"Here you go, Hallie. You don't want to lose this, so take special care that you don't misplace it when you unpack. It includes your daily schedule and, most important, the dining hall schedule. Be sure you make it for meals. After hours the kitchen is locked up tighter than Alcatraz."

"There will be plenty of choices for her, correct?" Mom asks.

"She's vegetarian," Dad adds, lowering his voice to a whisper. He hates that I'm vegetarian. He doesn't understand how anyone can survive without meat. Maybe it's my hedge witch ancestry, but I have a thing for organically grown vegetables. It's one of the many things Kendall used to tease me about.

Miss A gives a double thumbs-up. "Yes, ma'am!"

She hands me a beaded lanyard that reminds me of

the necklace I got when we visited an Indian reservation in Louisiana. No two stones are the same, and they have a tribal look to them.

Hanging from the lanyard is an ID card. Dead center is a picture of me I've never seen, wearing the exact same shirt I'm wearing now. I mentally backtrack through the last few months. Did I try this shirt on before today? Did Mom take my picture? I know that I know that I *know* . . . I didn't put this shirt on before today. So that means they took this picture . . . today? How? When? And how'd it get on my badge so quickly?

Miss A leans forward and puts the lanyard around my neck. "Don't even think about walking out of your room without this. It's your key to everything—your room, the dining hall, the commissary, and your classes."

She's odd and kind of hard to take seriously, but I already like my dorm mother. I was terrified a controlling, power-hungry shrew would be in charge of my life. Miss A is the complete opposite of that nightmare.

"Heather, honey," she calls behind her. The most beautiful girl I've ever seen glides across the waxed hardwood floor. She's older than me, but not by much. Probably two or three years. The brilliant blond hair draped over her shoulder is shinier than silk. If going to Dowling does this to a girl, I'm all in.

"Yes, Miss A?" She smiles sweetly at my mom away from home.

"Can you please show the Simons to Hallie's room? She's in 128."

"128? That's my old room! You're going to love it! You have the thermostat, so you get to control the temperature for the even-numbered rooms in your wing."

I smile and nod, not sure how that makes the room special. But if Heather says it's good, who am I to argue?

Her smile sparkles, and she places a delicate hand over her heart. "I'm Heather Ellis, a Crafter." The word "crafter" is spoken with pride bordering on conceit.

"Lead the way, m'lady," Dad says, dipping into a deep bow to Heather. I roll my eyes, wishing I knew the spell to make myself invisible. Or make him mute.

Miss A chuckles, her laugh deep and loud, more of a boisterous belly laugh than a witch's cackle. I decide there's something genuinely good about her, and my entire body exhales.

Dad grabs both ends of the trunk, and we follow Heather down a wide hallway. The walls are a shiny dark wood that matches the floors. Between every door is a small, bare bulletin board with a handful of colorful tacks. We walk down the hallway, some doors open with girls inside, other doors closed, probably waiting for their new residents. The air vibrates with the buzz of nerves.

Heather points to room 125 when we pass it. "That's Miss A's room."

I could have guessed that, since it's the only room in the hallway with any sign of personality. Plastic butterflies and butterflies drawn on paper and butterflies cut from magazines are pinned to her bulletin board. There isn't a fraction of a centimeter that isn't covered. Hanging above her door are three wind chimes. All with butterflies on them.

"Interesting," Mom says, letting her hand softly tap the lowest wind chime as she walks by.

My eyes focus on the iridescent wings of the wind chime's butterflies. Wings that look like they're moving, wings in flight. But just as quickly as the wings began moving, they return to their plastic, frozen-in-space position. I blink a few times, not sure what I'm seeing is real—it must be nerves.

I half-run to catch up with my parents, happy to put some space between me and Miss A's weird wind chimes.

Heather stops in front of the last door on the left. "Here we are."

She points to the silver strip just above the handle. "Your ID has a magnetic stripe on it that you'll slide here to unlock the door, just like a hotel key card."

I swipe the card through the metal strip. A green light flashes three times, and a soft click tells me the door's unlocked.

"You're already a master." Heather pats her dainty hand on my back before pushing the door open. I squint through my glasses into the black hole that is now my room.

Heather giggles. "Go on in. It's not a black hole. Promise."

At her echo of my own thoughts, I spin to look at her. Heather keeps the Tour-Guide-Barbie smile on her face. It's a common phrase, right? She might use that phrase with everyone.

Baby step after baby step, I draw farther into the dark room, unsure what to expect. Bunk beds? A mattress on the floor? Or will it be more like the prison cells I've seen on TV, with a bed of concrete and a metal toilet between the roommates' beds?

"I'm sorry, Hallie. Let me turn the light on for you." With a snap of Heather's pink-tipped fingers, fluorescent light floods the room, and I stop, dead still. Did she just *snap* the lights on?

"So?" she asks. "What do you think?"

In a room the size of a postage stamp, there's a twin bed on either side of the room, covered in a fluffy black-and-white floral quilt. Each bed has two overstuffed pillows that beg to be slept on. There are two small desks between the beds for us to work on. Tall lamps with black lampshades, and an organizer with pens, pencils, and highlighters, stand at attention. A small dresser is on the wall at the end of the bed. The dresser would be the perfect spot for a television if they weren't forbidden.

It's all very . . . surprising. In a good way.

"What a room, Hal! My college dorm wasn't nearly this nice!" Mom walks past me and sits on a bed, pushing on the springs, my duffel bag still on her shoulder. "It's soft, just like your bed at home."

Home. The word alone is a little confusing now. Where exactly is my home?

Heather takes a trunk handle and helps Dad haul the truck into the room. "Your mom picked the right bed for you. The other bed is directly under the air vent. Not good."

I smile at Heather, fascinated with her temperature-control obsession.

"Let's put the trunk here," she says, walking to the foot of the bed. "You'll need it for storage. Closet space is wretched."

Dad occupies himself with making sure the trunk is perfectly centered. Presentation is everything.

Heather walks to the small hallway just inside the doorway. "Here's the closet," she says, pulling the sliding door open. "See what I mean? And remember, you have to share this with your roommate. Most girls put their uniforms in here and keep their other clothes in the dresser."

I peek inside the teeny tiny closet, more appropriate for holding a few coats than the wardrobes of two girls. She was right. It won't even hold the minuscule wardrobe I brought with me.

"This is your bathroom. You'll share it with your roommate too. It's smart to figure out early who's going to take their shower first. Oh, and you'll want to limit your showers. Otherwise the second person showering will have absolutely no hot water. It lasts ten minutes, tops."

"Thanks for the insider information," Dad says, finally

satisfied with the position of the trunk. "See, Hallie? I was right. Life is all about—"

"Who you know," I mutter, my face roasting.

I thought telling my parents good-bye would be hard, but I think I'm ready to see them go.

Heather giggles. "You're funny," she says to my dad in a way that coming from anyone else would sound like a Kendall-worthy insult.

Looking at me, she points to an ancient corded phone hanging on the wall across from the closet. "You can use this phone to call people in the building, but it doesn't dial out. You can call room to room by dialing the room number. I'm in room 205 on the second floor. Just give me a shout if you have a question and can't find Miss A."

Dad whips a pad of sticky notes from his pocket and scribbles on it. He sticks the note next to the phone. "So you don't forget Heather's number," he says, undeniably happy that his resourcefulness has once again saved the day.

"You have plenty of time to walk around the main building before invocation. Take your map with you and just get a feel of the building. The older girls arrive a little before five."

"Those poor girls. They'll never get unpacked before invocation," Mom says.

Heather shakes her head, bright smile shining. "You'd be surprised how quickly it goes." She turns her attention back to me. "Feel free to roam around. We just ask that you stay on your floor."

I wasn't planning on climbing the stairs uninvited, but now I'm curious. "Why?"

Her smile slides into a grin. "It's for your protection. You'll understand soon."

I nod, realization settling in my bones like a lead weight. I'm really and truly going to live at a school for witches, a school full of scary secrets. Without my parents.

Heather looks around the room, then closes the closet door. "I think that's about it. Do you have any questions before I go?"

I look at Mom, then Dad, both of them shaking their heads.

"How do I call home?" I ask.

Heather slaps her forehead. "Great question! I can't believe I forgot to tell you."

I follow Heather to the door and look to where she points down the hall. "See that little hallway right next to Miss A's room?"

I lean forward to get a better look. "Sure," I lie.

"There's a phone in that little hallway. They say there's a five-minute limit, but no one really watches the clock."

My parents press against me, eyes following Heather's pointed finger.

She steps farther out the doorway. "If you don't need me, I'll leave you to unpack."

Mom beats Dad to the closing handshake. "Thank you, Heather," she says with such gratitude, you'd think Heather had just pulled me from a burning building. "You've been so helpful."

Heather's smile lights up the hallway. "It's been my pleasure, Mrs. Simon. Nice to meet all of you." She pulls her hand from Mom's grasp, then begins walking down the hall. After a few steps she stops abruptly, turns around, and calls out, "See you at invocation, Hallie. Five o'clock sharp."

"Okay," I call back with an awkward wave. And there's a scared little part of me that wishes Heather would come back and teach me some do-or-die Dowling survival skills.

Because without them, Dowling's going to put me in the cauldron and turn me into next week's stew.

Three

Mom stretches five minutes of unpacking into twenty. When she can't find anything else to fluff, fix, or freshen, she stares and stares and stares at me, and I think I see the hint of tears in her eyes. Like she'll never see me again.

Dad squints at the alarm clock I've put on my desk. 3:32 p.m. "Well, kiddo, guess it's time for us to hit the road."

He puts his arm around Mom's shoulders and squeezes.

I grab them for a quick group hug, then step back, terrified I'll actually start crying. Mom visibly wills herself to be strong, to hold it together until she can get into the car. I look so much like her—same brown hair, same brown eyes, same brown glasses. I wonder if my expression, like hers, is paralyzing panic.

"Maybe we should stay until your roommate gets here." The desperation in her voice makes my heart cramp.

I shake my head at her offer. "I'll be fine." I grab the map and schedule Mom neatly laid on my desk. "I've got a lot to look over."

Mom nods, pulls me in for one last hug. "I love you, sweetie."

Dad walks Mom to the door, practically dragging her like a stubborn dog on a leash. I give him a grateful smile. If they don't leave in the next fifteen seconds, I'll start a crying jag that will leave me blotchy, puffy, and stuffy. Definitely not how I intend to meet my roommate.

I follow them to the hallway, now crowded with families being escorted by Heather-like students. "Stop worrying. I'm okay."

Dad puts his free hand on my shoulder, probably afraid to let go of Mom. "You're the first Simon in five generations to attend Dowling. You have the opportunity to create a name for yourself. Make us proud."

"Make *yourself* proud," Mom pipes in.

They're both right, of course. In the world of witchcraft only the strong succeed. I suspect Dad wishes he'd been born a girl, or at least been born with the ability to become a hedge witch like Great-great-grandmother Elsa. But our lineage is passed on woman to woman or man to man, so Dad's ability to be a witch could never happen. Male witches descend from men and go to a different school. Despite the endless ways my dad embarrasses me, I love him. I want to make him—and myself—proud.

Wordlessly they walk down the long hallway until they get to Miss A's door. Dad stops, points to something next to her door, and I realize it's the student phone. He pulls the receiver into the hallway and waves it at me. I give him a quick thumbs-up, walk into my room, shut the door, and cry.

I'm washing my face when I hear the door unlock. I freeze, wanting to hide and check out my roommate before meeting her. But even I won't do something so silly. This is a new me. A new beginning.

I could be meeting my first real best friend.

I fly to my bed and sit cross-legged with the map and schedule in front of me, as if I've been here all day. As if I don't care who my roommate is. The door opens, and Heather enters the room.

"Your roommate's here!"

I peer around Heather, but all I can see is a large framed picture in front of my roommate. Guess she took that whole "decorations allowed" thing pretty seriously. I look at the two throw pillows on my bed and the pair of framed pictures on my dresser and instantly wish I'd brought more.

My roommate walks inside and lowers the frame to the floor, and every cell in my body freezes when our eyes lock.

No. Freaking. Way.

I know that flawless face, that not-quite-smiling mouth, that perfectly highlighted blond hair.

Even in the same outfit I'm wearing and without makeup, she looks superior.

She breathes deeply, evil eyes glaring. If she's as stunned as me, she's hiding it perfectly. "Hallie."

I don't give in to my usual habit of looking away, and instead stare straight into her ice-blue judgmental eyes. "Kendall," I say, mimicking her I'm-too-good-for-you tone.

"Wait," Heather says, looking back and forth between us. "You two actually know each other?"

Kendall rolls her eyes. "Only forever."

"How lucky is that?" Heather says. "You can help each other learn the Dowling ropes!"

"So lucky," Kendall says, sarcasm dripping from her lips. It's the same tone she's used with me for years.

"This might be a first in Dowling history. I've never heard of roommates who knew each other before coming here."

I keep my face smiling despite every fight-or-flight instinct screaming at me to run. Run away from Dowling. Run away from Kendall. Run away from my *karama*. Suddenly, starting over seems like a really bad idea.

Some girls are destined to inherit family fortunes. Me? I get to be part of centuries-old witchcraft practices and room with my only enemy.

We were best friends until third grade, when I got glasses and Kendall decided cool kids didn't. She took all our friends with her, and I've basically been a loner since then. Kendall, however, continued her rapid rise on the popularity ladder, never once looking back at me and our friendship.

Kendall's parents hustle into the room, laboring with a bulky trunk and overstuffed duffel bag. The last time I was at the Scott house, three years ago, Mom had to pick me up at two in the morning after Kendall and her cronies locked me in a dark closet until I begged to go home.

"Whew," Mrs. Scott says, releasing the trunk and putting a hand to her back. "That's one heck of a long hallway!"

Dad's voice echoes in my head. *Kill them with kindness.*

"Hello, Mr. and Mrs. Scott," I say, standing to extend my hand for a firm handshake.

Dad would be so proud.

Mr. Scott is the first to speak, looking down at me over his glasses with cold eyes before shaking my hand. "Hallie. So good to see you again." His words are nice enough, but he says them with the gravity usually reserved for devastating life-changing events. Like dropping-your-cell-phone-in-the-toilet kind of devastating.

Kendall's mom walks a few steps closer, then realizes she knows me. The color fades from her face, and she stammers with a series of uhs, ums, and huhs. It'd be funny if I wasn't feeling the same way.

I cram the mounting hysteria way down deep inside me. There's no way I'm letting Kendall see how rattled I am.

I silently thank my parents for making sure we were here early. Saying good-bye to my parents in front of Kendall would have been more embarrassing than the time I puked in gym after losing the one-mile race. To Kendall.

Obviously sensing the tension, Heather's once sunshiny

smile is forced, her eyes too wide. She races Kendall and her parents through a tour of the room. I'm secretly satisfied when she doesn't share the helpful hints about the shower and phone.

"Parents have to be gone by four o'clock sharp," she says apologetically. Like it's her fault they showed up right at the last possible minute. That's exactly how Kendall used to show up for class, sliding in just as the bell rang. Every class. Every day. I always wondered what she did between classes that made her so late.

"Invocation's at five. Don't be late. Headmistress Fallon detests tardiness."

Punctuality is totally my thing. Kendall? Not so much. "No problem. Can you tell me where it is?" I ask.

"Go back to the lobby, then follow the crowd of girls to the Gathering Circle. Can't miss it."

Heather waves and walks out, the door closing behind her automatically. I try to remember if that happened the last time she left, but I specifically remember having to push the door closed. Is that the way things are here? Doors open and close without assistance? That could totally come in handy.

"Can I help you get unpacked?" I ask, more out of polite habit than generosity.

Kendall doesn't look at me, speak to me, or acknowledge me in any way. She's quite the expert at that irritating
little skill.

I lie back on my supercomfy bed to read the map and
schedule. Again. I'm determined to memorize it so I don't
constantly look lost.

I sneak quick glances at Kendall unpacking. She carefully places familiar lime-green throw pillows on her bed.
I giggle on the inside. Kendall will be horrified when she
realizes we brought identical decorations.

Her mom unpacks the trunk, putting clothes in the
dresser and cramming the closet. Guess I won't be hanging *my* uniforms.

Her dad centers the large frame on the wall above her
dresser. From where I'm lying, I can perfectly see the collage
of at least a hundred pictures of Kendall and her friends,
a.k.a. my tormenters, in identical pouty poses in different
places. The movie theater. The mall. The classroom . . .
where phones aren't even allowed! Instead of escaping my
enemies, I'll have to see them every single day.

Out of forty-eight new Seekers entering Dowling, I
had to get paired with the horrid and venomous Kendall. I
shouldn't be surprised she's here. Of all the people I know,

she's the one most likely to carry the evil-witch gene.

At 3:58, Kendall tells her parents it's time for them to leave. Unlike my own mother, Mrs. Scott doesn't stall or fret. She gives Kendall a brisk hug, more like a coach might do before a big game than a mother leaving her daughter at a boarding school. For witches.

On second thought, if I was Kendall's mother, I'd be kind of excited about leaving Kendall here too.

"Be good, and please, be on time. For once." Her mom narrows her eyes in warning.

"Don't forget to call," her dad says, patting his daughter's shoulder awkwardly, as if showing affection is foreign to him. If I didn't know how awful Kendall is, I'd feel sorry for her. Kendall walks to the door and opens it wide. "I'll call," she says quietly. I'm struck by the softness in her voice, a side of her I haven't seen in years. Maybe ever. Is it possible she's nervous too?

She stands in the doorway, watching her parents leave. I sit up in bed, thinking maybe, just maybe, Kendall will attempt to be civil now that we're stuck together and all we have is each other.

Right here, right now, we are equal.

She shuts the door behind her parents. It doesn't close

automatically, making me second-guess what I thought I saw when Heather left the room. Kendall goes to the bathroom and locks the door behind her. I fight the urge to put my ear to the door to see if she's crying. But when she comes out seconds later, her eyes are clear, every hair on her head positioned perfectly.

Of course she wasn't crying. That would require her to have a heart.

"Funny about our pillows," I say, nervous laughter breaking my words. "They're exactly the same."

Silence.

Why am I even talking to her?

She yanks the chair from her desk and straddles it, facing me. Heaving a big sigh, she pulls the lanyard off her neck and tosses it carelessly onto her desk. I stop myself from suggesting she put a tack on the wall beside her bed to hang it on like I did.

"Let's get one thing straight, Hallie," she says, her voice quiet, mean. I brace myself for what she's about to say, for what she's about to call me. What's it going to be today? Four-eyes? Geek? Loser? Freak?

I don't say anything, just push my glasses up.

"Nothing has changed. We may be in a new school

with new people and new teachers, but you're still you and I'm still me. You and I," she says, pointing back and forth between us, "are just roommates. We will *never* be friends."

So much for new beginnings.

"I wouldn't want it any other way," I tell her, wondering if Miss A can move me to a different room. The janitor's closet, maybe.

Kendall pushes out of the chair, lies on the bed, and closes her eyes.

I stare in shock, lie back on my own bed, and wonder what I did to deserve the curse of Kendall.

Four

I leave we'll-never-be-friends Kendall on her bed and my dorky glasses on my dresser. The hallway is more alive than when I arrived, each girl wearing identical nervous smiles. Roommates stand close together, forging small but coveted alliances. Jealousy twists in my chest. Why did I have to get stuck with Kendall? Perfect, popular, petty Kendall.

Straightening my lanyard, I pull my shoulders back and take a deep, slow breath. The trip down the hall feels like a walk through the social gauntlet—a big smile here, a polite hello there, a sweet grin in between. Move over, Miss Congeniality . . . Hallie's here!

At the end of the hallway, a girl walks out of her room alone. Two long, red braids frame her tense face.

I slow my steps and dare myself to be more outgoing.

"Time to look around, I guess." I wave the map for unnecessary emphasis. Like she doesn't know what I mean by "look around."

She chews on her lip, nerves defying her attempt to look casual.

Maybe it's the braids, or the freckles dotting her nose, but she reminds me of a sweet, little farm girl.

Not a witch. Not by a long-handled broom.

"Want to explore Dowling with me?"

She smiles, mouth full of braces with neon-green rubber bands. "Sure."

I peek over her shoulder to look inside her room. "Should we ask your roommate to come with us?"

She shakes her head and shuts the door. No magical door here, either. A small bubble of hope bursts inside me. I was kind of wishing those were real.

"Nah," she says. "She knows her way around."

My mind trips over her comment like it's a speed bump. How does her roommate know her way around? Everyone on this floor is new.

I ignore the urge to ask her about it, and shake it off. I just met her; questions can come later. "Okay, cool. I'm Hallie. Hallie Simon."

"Ivy Oliver," she says, her voice steady, all trace of anxiety gone or well hidden.

Because she's taller than me, I have to work to match her steps. We go past the lobby, where only a handful of adults and a few older girls, Heather included, are talking quietly. They must be waiting for the next group to arrive.

Ivy stops in the large open area off the lobby. "Where do you want to go first?"

I glance at the map like I don't have it memorized. Gathering Circle on the left, dining room straight ahead, library on the right, and some specialty rooms in the basement. I don't know what's so special about those rooms, but I don't do basements unless there's an F-5 tornado. They make me feel like I'm being buried alive in a damp coffin.

"Looks like we'll come to the Gathering Circle first," I say.

We walk in silence with other girls from our hallway, some stopping to look at the oversize portraits hanging on the walls. I'm curious about them too, but Ivy doesn't seem interested, so we keep on walking.

"My sister graduated from Dowling a couple of years ago," she says. "But I've never been past the lobby."

"You're lucky. I'm the first girl in five generations to attend Dowling."

"You're the first girl in your family in five generations?" Ivy asks.

"I wish I had someone to talk to who's been here before," I say.

Ivy shakes her head. "Wouldn't matter. They can't tell you anything, and they never show you any cool tricks. It's against the code." Her dark green eyes roll expertly. "Whatever that means."

We stop inside the Gathering Circle and let our eyes adjust to the dim lighting.

"Wow," Ivy whispers.

I nod, not trusting my voice to be quiet enough for this space. You can just tell that in this room, no one speaks above a hush.

The room is sunken, with a large, triangular stage at the bottom. Its bare wooden floor is polished, patiently awaiting its next speaker. There are no microphones, no stools, no lecture stands. In the center stands a gold, triangular table holding a half dozen crystal containers with various colored liquids that swirl like they're being stirred by an invisible straw. A small bronze vase containing some type of herb catches my attention. I squint my eyes, trying to see better.

Surrounding the stage are six circular rows of seats, each row lower than the one before. Kind of like a very fancy, circular movie theater. The whole thing reminds me of a big dart board, and the stage is the bull's-eye.

White candles of every size in glass containers hang from thick chains, giving the room a calm, peaceful feeling.

My mind buzzes with questions. Questions I'm not sure I want answers to.

What kinds of events take place in here?

What exactly is in the crystal containers?

What are we expected to do with them?

Ivy gives me a friendly shoulder-to-shoulder bump. "Don't look so worried. We'll be fine."

I force my face to relax. "Oh, yeah. Fine."

I follow Ivy out of the Gathering Circle and stop at the first portrait I see.

"Guess these are all the important witches who went to Dowling," Ivy says. "Cool, huh?"

"Very. I kind of have a thing for history."

Ivy's freckled nose wrinkles. "Eww. Really?"

My heart sinks a little, making me wish I could turn

back time and take back those words. There are definitely cooler things I could have said. Things like "If you're into that kind of thing." Or "Yeah, I guess," with a bored shrug.

The woman in the portrait doesn't look like a witch. She looks more like a movie star with jet-black hair in long perfect curls. Her pale blue eyes sparkle with life, and there's a tiny little snicker lifting one corner of her full red lips. You can tell she was the kind of woman who knew things—and did things—she probably shouldn't have.

Ivy's voice breaks my trance. *"High Priestess Dannabelle Grimm, 1845–1851."*

"I wonder what she was like, what her powers were," I say, more to myself than Ivy. Could she create a tornado in an attic?

I make a mental note of Dannabelle's name so I can look her up. Assuming I'll be allowed to use the library.

Our attention is pulled from Dannabelle by squeals of happiness followed by somber reprimands floating from the lobby.

"Let's go see," Ivy says, a zing of excitement in her voice.

I linger at the portrait a few more seconds before following Ivy. Even as we move farther away, I can't shake the feeling that Dannabelle's watching me, that her eyes are moving as I move, that she wants me to come back to her.

Ivy freezes, and I run into her rigid body. I look over her shoulder and blink hard.

The lobby is a frenzy of activity. Girls hugging, teachers passing out schedules, and family trunks whizzing up the stairs. On their own. Trunks are literally gliding up the stairs, a foot or two off the ground.

Unattended.

Like they know where they're going.

I clap both hands over my mouth and attempt to swallow the panic stuck in my throat. So much for the new, totally-in-control Hallie.

Some of the girls look at us, wave like there's nothing unusual happening, and go back to whatever they were doing.

A blur of multicolored fabric steals my gaze from the staircase. My body goes soft with relief when I realize it's Miss A.

"Now, girls, don't be startled," she says, hurrying toward us with a shiny smile. "This kind of thing happens a lot around here, but if you ask me . . . ," she says with a wink, "the girls are showing off for you. This is their first year as Crafters, and I suppose they're just happy they aren't the new kids anymore."

"Crafters?" I ask.

Miss A takes my hand and pats Ivy on the shoulder. "You know, Crafters. It's what you'll be when you finish your year as a Seeker."

Ivy's now glassy eyes squint like she's trying to see something a mile away. "You mean, next year . . . Next year . . . We?" Her once steady voice now shakes like she's talking into a fan, and her face is a weird grayish color.

Miss A answers Ivy's unasked question. "Next year that will be you."

Ivy looks at me, shakes her head slowly, then crumbles like a crashing Jenga tower.

Miss A flicks her fingers like she's trying to shake water off her hands. Before Ivy slumps to the ground in a heap, her body freezes in place. As if someone pushed the pause button on a movie.

I stare, wide-eyed, at Miss A, at Ivy suspended midfall, and force myself to breathe.

In.

Out.

In.

Out.

"I . . . How d-d-did you . . . ," I stammer, stumbling over my thoughts.

"Sugar, you're in a school for witches. How do you think I did it?" Miss A gives me a look, like we're sharing a forbidden piece of gum in church.

"Right." Reading about magic in books seems safe, kind of exciting. Seeing it in person is mind-warping.

Am I really going to have that kind of power? Do I *want* it?

Miss A lowers her head, her eyes intense. A curl pops loose from the cluster of bobby pins in her hair, as if it, too, wants to see what's happening. The curl moves, grows fatter, and twists. I lean closer to see what it really is. Did that curl have eyes? Miss A swipes her hand through her hair, and whatever I saw disappears.

Breathe, Hallie.

In.

Out.

Miss A's voice is surprisingly stern and low when she speaks. "My precious little Seeker, wake. From this fall no memory you'll take."

Miss A twirls her hands upward, and in an instant Ivy is back on her feet. Her innocent eyes find mine.

"Are you okay?" she asks me. "You don't look so good."

I don't scream, "Of course I'm not okay!" And I don't run to the phone outside Miss A's room, call my parents, and beg them to take me home. One look at Miss A's meaningful expression, and I know what I have to do.

I lie to my only friend at Dowling. "Couldn't be better."

Five

I grab Ivy's hand, partly because I'm worried she'll faint again and partly because I'm worried I might pass out myself.

Miss A puts her hands on our backs, leading us away from the flying trunks. "Why don't you two go on into the GC and get comfy?"

Ivy and I share confused looks.

"GC, Gathering Circle, to-may-to, to-mah-to," Miss A says, pointing to the room we just left. "It's always smart to get there a little early before it gets too crowded. I'll be there in two shakes."

With a couple of quick pats to our backs, she half-shoves us into the line of girls walking into the GC.

Closer to the entrance I see Kendall. She's smiling

from ear to ear and talking closely with the girl next to her.
I should have known Kendall would find someone else to
buddy with. Anyone but me. And I can just tell from looking at the other girl that they are as perfect together as
Thelma and Louise.

"There's my roommate," Ivy mumbles. "Nice to see her
highness decided to leave the dungeon."

I follow Ivy's stare and realize she's talking about
Kendall's friend. "Her? The one next to the blonde with
her arms crossed?"

Ivy nods, eyes squinted into angry little slits.

"Why don't you like her?"

Eyes wide, she gawks at me. "Hello, that's Zena."

I shake my head. "No clue what you're talking
about."

We take a few steps forward, but Ivy keeps her eyes
pinned on me. "Are you serious? Have you honestly not
done a single second of research on this place?"

"Umm . . ." Yeah. Looking back, I probably should've
done that. In fact, it's totally unlike me to *not* research
every aspect of Dowling before arriving. I guess I really
never thought I'd actually come.

She sighs deeply. "My roommate is *the* Zena Fallon."

"As in Headmistress Fallon?"

"Bingo," Ivy says. "Zena is her daughter. Zena thought she'd have her choice of rooms and that she'd be allowed to live without a roommate. She's lived at Dowling with her mother her entire life, but this is the first year she'll live at Dowling as a student."

I nod, trying to take it all in. The headmistress has a daughter? And we have to go to school with her?

"She threw a total tantrum when Miss A told her that she'd be rooming with me."

"Jeez," I whisper, moving even closer to the entrance.

"She wanted to be in the last room and alone. But her mother didn't have the heart to break the news to her beforehand, so I was lucky enough to witness the entire scene with Miss A. She swore she'd never leave the room, and Miss A told her to build a bridge and get over it."

I giggle at that, and Ivy laughs too.

"The girl she's with?" I say. "That's my roommate."

"You can't be serious."

"The worst part is that she's just like Zena."

"No one's as bad as Zena," Ivy says, head shaking as we clear the doorway to the darkened room.

"Trust me. I've known Kendall my whole life. She's worse than Lucifer himself."

Inside the entrance to the Gathering Circle, we're stopped by a woman in a dark red, floor-length dress. She is as perfect as a person could ever be. Flawless everything—skin, hair, figure, makeup. Even the look on her face is the perfect mix of warm but serious, gentle but strong.

"Welcome, Seeker Hallie," she says, placing her hand on my left shoulder. I stand frozen, speechless. It's like a greeting you'd receive from a martian. I suppose I should be used to people I've never met knowing my name around here, but it still creeps me out.

The woman moves her hand from my shoulder to Ivy's. "Welcome, Seeker Ivy."

She dismisses us with a nod.

"Awkward," Ivy half-sings, half-whispers.

A student about the same age as Heather hands us each a slip of paper. She doesn't utter a sound, just smiles and nods. It's like they have a whole other language here.

I look down at the paper. *Row 6, Seat 21.*

I glance down at Ivy's. Same row, seat 22. Finally some good luck.

We sit in the top row of polished wooden benches,

almost near the aisle. From where we're sitting, we can see the triangular stage in the center of the room perfectly. The candlelit room fills slowly.

Kendall and Zena are sitting almost directly across from us in the circle. Zena looks like Kendall's complete opposite. Different hair color, eye color, even the coloring of their skin is different. But everything else about them is eerily similar. Same snarky smile, same judgmental eyes. Familiar insecurity squeezes my empty stomach.

"Weird how that woman knew our names, right?" Ivy whispers.

"And what was with the hand on the shoulder? I half-expected her to say 'May the force be with you.'"

Ivy giggles quietly, and I let my body relax just a bit. Rooming with Kendall is not what I wanted, but at least Ivy seems normal. Well, as normal as a preteen witch can be.

Nearly every seat on the top row is filled when Miss A enters the room and sits in one of six chairs on the triangular stage. Silence follows, as if everyone in the room instinctively knows something is about to happen.

A single file line of girls walks softly into the room. The girls' eyes are straight ahead, and their steps are perfectly in sync. With the grace of ballerinas they slide into their seats in the row beneath ours. A woman much younger and much less colorful than Miss A sits on the stage.

The same routine is repeated until all six rows circling the stage are filled. It's obvious now that we're sitting in groups based on our levels. The Seekers are on the top row, evident from our wide eyes and nervous fidgeting. The girl who escorted us to my room, Heather, is almost directly in front of me, one row down.

Somehow the flames on the candles dim. In fact, I can barely see any flame on the wicks, and we are shrouded in almost complete darkness. A candle on the stage lights, instantly brightening the area. I feel like I'm watching a magic show at the circus. It's hard to believe this is my new world.

The woman in red who welcomed us at the door practically floats to the stage, then stands behind the table holding the lit candle. The liquids and herbs I noticed earlier are still in their unique containers. Again, I wish I'd worn my glasses so I could see them better.

The woman is illuminated in such a way that is seems more like a dream than reality, and I can't take my eyes off her. Fair-skinned with shoulder-length nearly black hair so shiny it looks like silk, she reminds me of Snow White.

"Welcome, sisters of Dowling," she says, her voice soft but commanding and just loud enough to be heard without a microphone. "I am so pleased to see you all. Seekers, let me introduce myself. My name is Veronica Fallon, and I have been Dowling's headmistress for thirteen years. It was my privilege to welcome each of you today." She smiles knowingly. "I assure you, this year will be like no other for you."

Nearly every non-Seeker in the room nods in agreement, some giggling, some snickering.

"But you are not alone. Dowling is truly a sisterhood. And tonight we celebrate the beginning of a new year."

The headmistress holds her hands over the containers like she's warming her hands over a fire. As if on cue, every item on the table comes to life. The liquids sparkle and dance, and you can practically hear the herb singing in its dish.

Headmistress Fallon speaks more loudly, her eyes seeming to make contact with each and every person in the room at once. She picks up a small wooden stick—her wand—that looks so much like the one in my family trunk,

I half-wonder if Kendall stole it and gave it to her. She raises her hands above her head like a conductor about to begin a symphony, and the flame of the candle in front of her grows to at least two feet. In the sudden brightness of the enormous flame, she speaks.

"Dowling sisters, your powers proclaim,
your right of lineage by Saffra's name.
A witch can give success in love,
curse or bless through Saffra above.
Speak to beasts and spirits alike,
command the weather, cast out a blight.
Read the heavens and stars of the night,
divine the future and give good advice.
Conjure treasure and bring fortune to bear,
heal the sick and kill despair.
This is your birthright to have and to share,
blessings, my sisters,
may the spirits be fair."

She lowers her hands, and the flame of the candle lowers once again.

My heart is racing more than I'd admit, and the creep

factor has me picking at my fingernails. Flying suitcases, magic candles, martian greetings? Is this really who I am? Who I want to be? What was so wrong with my invisible little life? It might have been boring, but at least it was safe and predictable.

"Your life at Dowling will never be boring, my Seekers."

Whaaaaat? My head shoots up at the echo of my thoughts. The headmistress is looking at me like I'm the only person in the room. Like she's reaching inside my brain and snatching my thoughts. Like she's trying to convince me that being at Dowling is a blessing.

"Dowling *will* be your life's greatest blessing."

I stop breathing and squeeze my eyes shut.

Get out of my head.

Get out of my head.

As I open my eyes, the candles around the room light again, as if they're on magical timers.

The headmistress finally takes her penetrating stare off me. "As is tradition, we will recite the Dowling Code. Seekers, please listen carefully, as you, too, will be required to memorize and understand its meaning."

In chorus, the other students and adults in the room speak.

The XYZs of Being Wicked

"*Delicias fuge ne frangaris crimine, verum*
Coelica tu quareas, ne male dipereas;
Respicias tua, non cujusvis quaerito gesta
Carpere, sed laudes, nec preme veridicios;
Judicio fore te praesentem conspice toto."

"What you just heard, Seekers, is the code all Dowling students live by. Not just within these doors but long after they've left our campus. Translated it means:

Shun pleasures of the flesh, lest you be broken by crime;
Seeks things of the heavens, lest your end be an evil one;
Consider your own deeds, and do not seek to slander
   someone else's,
But praise them, and do not suppress those who speak
   the truth;
Always realize that you must stand before judgment.

I almost giggle at the thought of Kendall following any part of that code, especially praising others and speaking the truth. That's definitely not something she's accustomed to doing.

The headmistress continues. "There are several rules

you should be aware of at Dowling, Seekers. Rules that have consequences if broken. If the infraction is severe enough, the punishment could result in expulsion from Dowling, and even expulsion of your entire family line for future generations."

She holds up one perfectly manicured finger. "Rule one. No dark magic. There is enough evil in this world without our help. Our purpose is to make the world a better-balanced and more harmonious place."

A second finger goes up. "Rule two. No cheating. You are all incredibly intelligent, so this should be absolutely no problem."

Three fingers. "Last but not least, rule three. No stealing. We live in a community at Dowling. We must honor the belongings of everyone in this building. If you need something, ask. But *never* steal." Her eyes are serious, almost frighteningly so.

Three rules? Piece of cake.

"It may seem like a piece of cake compared to the rules at your old schools," she says, "but it is harder than you think."

Again my eyes bulge when I hear my thoughts repeated by the headmistress. This time she isn't looking at me.

"Seekers, there are two rituals that must be performed tonight, before you enter your first class and before you begin learning about your gifts. The first is the Self-Dedication Right, and the second is your acceptance of your family's Book of Shadows. Every other girl in this room had to go through these same rituals when they were Seekers. And now? Now it is your turn."

Why do I feel like I'm the only one who's shocked by the things we see here? Have other families prepared their daughters while mine did not?

The headmistress continues, her voice smooth and confident. "Please locate the paper under your seat." Under my seat? I didn't see anything there before, but who am I to second-guess how things work at witch school?

Seriousness blankets the room. The giggling and whispering heard earlier is gone. The room is stone-cold silent.

"Prepare to commit yourself to the Dowling coven with a deep, cleansing breath." The room inhales and exhales in unison.

Satisfied we've breathed properly, she continues. "Please read along with me." And I do, because what other choice do I have?

"O Mother Saffra,
answerer of all mysteries;
In this place of power, I open myself to your essence.
In this place and in this time I am changed."

I glance at the girls around me. Everyone appears to be reading. The headmistress pauses, taking a deep, slow breath before continuing.

"I breathe your energies into my body,
mixing them with mine,
that I may see the divine in nature,
nature in the divine,
and divinity within myself and all else.
O Great Saffra,
make me one with your essence."

I wonder if anyone else is as confused as I am. What's an essence, and why do I want to be one with someone else's?

Headmistress Fallon's voice interrupts my near-shock silence. "Congratulations, ladies. Your place here is your *karama. Karama* means 'destiny.' It's your predetermined path."

The headmistress scans the room with her eyes, warmly and silently welcoming us to the coven.

"It's time now for you to receive your Book of Shadows. If you will look under your chair, you will find your family's book."

I know my Book of Shadows is in my room. Or it was an hour ago.

I freeze in totally freaked-out shock when I see the book under my chair. I guess I shouldn't be surprised they were able to get it from me without me knowing, but I am. Pulling it to my lap, I open and see my great-great-grandmother's inscription on the inside cover. The same one I saw in the attic. This whole witch school thing is going to take some getting used to.

"It is customary to bless your Book of Shadows," the headmistress says. "Please place your book on your lap and your hands on its cover."

Everyone follows her directions silently.

"Repeat after me," she says.

"Elements, protect this book
from wondering eyes and prying looks."

The headmistress pauses while we recite her words, then continues.

"And fill it with thine ancient power,
in this right and ready hour."

"Congratulations, Seekers," she says. "The Book of Shadows in your hands is now yours. May the blessings of your ancestors guide you all of your days."

I open the book again, flip through a few pages, then close it carefully. I am officially a Dowling Seeker.

I'm really and truly going to be a witch.

The headmistress addresses the dorm moms on the stage. "Please escort your girls to the dining room."

One by one the other women on the stage lead their charges from the room. I can't help but wonder what they'll serve us. Frogs? Rabbits? Children?

Finally Miss A stands and leads us from the room. As we enter the hallway, the hum of nervous chatter surrounds me. Ivy is talking about the headmistress and how beautiful she is, and all I can do is nod in agreement, my feet moving on autopilot while my mind races.

I can't stop thinking about the look the headmistress

gave me, as if she knows way more about me than I know about myself.

How does she know what I'm thinking?

I'll see that look in my dreams tonight. Maybe every night.

Kendall brushes past me with the headmistress's daughter like she has never laid eyes on me. Nothing has changed.

I thought my new life would be exciting, empowering, enchanting. But it has been the complete opposite in every possible way.

Maybe Dowling isn't my do-over after all.

Six

The smell of freshly baked bread hits my nose before we reach the dining room entrance. My stomach growls, reminding me I haven't eaten much of anything since breakfast.

Miss A leads us into a room with six long tables and a head table at the front of the room on a stage. It's the fanciest stage I've ever seen, with engraved woodwork on either side and black velvet curtains hanging down, held back with gold ropes.

Just as we sat by levels in the Gathering Circle, we also sit by levels in the dining room. The Seeker table is the first on the left. I follow Ivy closely to make sure we sit together. But as we near the table, I realize we have assigned seats. On each plate sits a small name card, our names written in perfect calligraphy to identify our seat. And beside each name is a number.

Panic tightens like hands around my throat. *Roommates* sit together.

Ivy looks at me, her green eyes mirroring my feelings. "No. I'm not sitting with that spoiled brat."

I shake my head. "I don't think we get a vote."

We walk together, looking at each name card carefully until we come to Ivy's name. Zena is already seated and looks like she'd rather be swimming in a pool full of rusty scissors than sitting next to her unwanted roommate.

"See you after dinner," I whisper, then walk on, looking at name cards while looking for Kendall. When I finally spot her, she's sitting about midtable on the opposite side, looking small and uncomfortable in the high-backed dining chair. Without Zena by her side, she looks more like everyone else—a little afraid, a little excited, and determined to deny it. Maybe she'll be more human now.

I walk around the table and pull my chair out, the heavy legs dragging across the floor loudly. Kendall shoots me a death glare. So much for being human. I ignore her and sit in the chair, then scoot closer to the table. More loud scraping.

Unlike everyone else's, the name card on my plate is green instead of white. I assume its how servers will know I'm vegetarian. The only one at the table, of course. Maybe in the whole room.

Kendall is to my right, and to my left is an empty seat for a student named Dru Goode. I say a silent prayer she's someone I can be friends with. Sitting next to the ice queen all year will make for very quiet meals.

I crane forward to see Ivy. From where I'm sitting, I can barely see her. In fact, if I didn't recognize her red braids, I probably wouldn't be able to pick her out.

Just as the doors to the dining room are being closed, a small girl slips through the just-big-enough crack between them like a fly zipping through the screen door at the last possible millisecond. Miss A, standing at the front of our table, smiles brightly at the girl and points toward me. This must be Dru.

When she reaches the chair next to me, she pulls it back, and—just as mine did—it drags loudly against the floor.

"Jeez," she mutters to herself.

I give her a small grin, relieved she's talking to me. Maybe I don't need Kendall after all. "Mine did the same thing."

She smiles back, but it's obvious she doesn't care what people think about her late—and loud—entrance. By the time Dru is settled, the dorm moms are seated at the head table, Headmistress Fallon in the center.

"Please bow your heads," the headmistress says.

Witches pray?

"Thank you, Saffra.
We ask you to bless us as we eat,
bless this food and bless the hands that prepared it.
May the words of our lips spring forth from
hearts of gratitude, and may we bless
others as we fellowship today."

I've got to find out who, or what, Saffra is. If I'm praying to her, or him, or it, I should know more about them.

The headmistress sits down, and a sea of waitstaff dressed in black enters the dining room like ants escaping a freshly kicked anthill.

I glance at Kendall, but her face is unreadable as she watches the flurry of activity and expertly pretends I don't exist.

"Did I miss anything?" Dru asks.

I shift my attention to the left and smile at the girl sitting next to me. Her tiny facial features make her look more like a well-tanned fairy than a witch. Even her dark black curls seem smaller than normal, each one happily springing from her head to frame her face. I know instantly she's going to be a friend.

"You didn't miss a thing," I reassure her.

A plate of spaghetti and meatballs is placed in front of Dru, and a meatball-free plate of spaghetti is laid in front of me. We both grab our forks and start twirling the pasta hungrily.

Dru talks faster than an auctioneer. "Where are you from? What's your room number? I'm in 122."

I open my mouth to answer her, but stop cold when my napkin slips out from under my silverware and moves from the table and into my lap in a perfect rectangle. I look at both Kendall and Dru to see if they saw it, and like me they're staring at their laps.

Dru nods and smiles. "Cool. I could totally get used to this magic stuff."

Kendall doesn't speak, just looks back at her plate and shoves the spaghetti around. Only the girls at the Seeker table are gawking in stunned silence; the other girls in the room are talking like normal, so I suppose this is something that happens at every meal.

I glance at the head table. Miss A is watching us, smiling in reassurance. It's little comfort, really. So many new—and seriously bizarre—things have already happened today, I can hardly imagine what else will happen.

"Why don't you have meatballs?" Dru asks, mouth full of food.

To my right my roommate whispers, "Freak."

I don't give her the satisfaction of a reply and focus on Dru.

"Vegetarian."

Dru shrugs, grinning. "That's kinda cool. My dad's, like, the opposite of that. He hates vegetables."

I watch Dru talk to everyone around her like she has known them all her entire life. She's exactly the kind of girl I planned to be at Dowling. Friendly, confident, and well liked.

Transforming myself into a new Hallie isn't going to be as easy as I thought, with my past sleeping in the bed next to me.

✳   ✳   ✳   ✳   ✳   ✳

I look at myself in the mirror. Teeth and hair brushed, face washed. I've completely run out of things to do.

No more stalling. The old Hallie avoided Kendall. The new Hallie doesn't.

I open the bathroom door and walk into the room.

Kendall is sitting on her bed, book open. She's still dressed in jeans and the red Dowling shirt. I grin to myself, happy I beat her to the bathroom.

"What are you reading?" I ask.

Silence.

I look at the folded red, navy, and white uniforms on my bed that were delivered while we were at dinner. I grab the small stack and place them in my dresser. "Guess I'll just put my uniforms in here. Closet looks a little crowded."

More silence.

I shake my head, frustrated by Kendall's rudeness. What did I ever do to her?

Determined to act like I don't care, I put my glasses on and take the large envelope from my top desk drawer so I can look at my schedule again. I crawl into bed and prop the pillows behind my back. Mom was right. The bed is comfortable, but it's not the same as my bed at home. There are no stuffed animals, no snoring dogs, and no posters on the wall. I can't hear Dad's favorite sports channel from the living room TV or the clanging of dishes as Mom cleans the kitchen.

Our room is silent.

An ache squeezes my chest. *Do not cry.*

Kendall tosses her book onto the desk carelessly, grabs pajamas from her dresser, and goes into the bathroom. I take a deep breath to calm myself down. I can't let Kendall see me upset.

I take my schedule from the envelope and review it again. I already have it half-memorized.

<u>Schedule for: Hallie Simon (Seeker, Room 128)</u>
1st period—History of Dowling
2nd period—English
3rd period—Math
Lunch
4th period—Elements of Witchcraft
5th period—Science
6th period—Study Hall
7th period—Personal Growth

I have no idea what I'll learn in the Elements of Witchcraft or Personal Growth classes, but it sure sounds better than band with my old music teacher. She was always screaming at us to sit up straight, even though we already were.

I wish I knew Kendall's schedule. The brown envelope is on her desk, and my fingers itch to open it. Sitting perfectly still, I listen to Kendall in the bathroom. The sink is on, so she'll be busy for a minute. I tiptoe out of bed and quietly put my fingers to the back of the envelope.

One more quick listen. The water is still on.

I open the envelope carefully and peek inside. I glance at the bathroom door, still closed. Kendall will kill me if she catches me. But this is a new day for Hallie Simon. No more wimping out.

I pull the top paper out, a centimeter at a time, until I can finally read it. I look at it carefully and compare it to my memory. Her schedule is identical to mine.

"Of course it is," I whisper to myself.

The water shuts off, and I frantically shove the paper back inside. But it gets hung on a loose paper clip, crinkling the paper.

Get the paper into the envelope.

Get the paper into the envelope.

I hear the flush of the toilet and see the bathroom light go out.

Out of time, I flip the brown envelope over and hope she doesn't look at it tonight. I can fix it while she's sleeping if she'll just ignore it for now. I hop into bed, grab my glasses, put my schedule back in front of my face, and ignore Kendall when she comes out of the bathroom.

She doesn't say anything, just climbs into bed and brushes her hair. Acting way calmer than I feel, I put my papers back into the envelope and grab one of my new books from the desk.

I pull my pillows down and slip farther into the sheets.

Kendall puts the brush on her desk, then eyes the envelope.

I hold my breath. *Please don't look at it.*

Her hand touches the envelope, and my meatless spaghetti threatens to reappear. I have to do something to distract her.

"Good night," I say, my voice perkier than the best cheerleader's in Texas.

She gives me a suspicious look, then climbs into bed.

She turns to her side, facing me, eyes closed. I feel my body relax, my heartbeat slow to a normal pace.

I can't believe my good luck. I open my book to the first page and begin reading.

Suddenly Kendall reaches up and turns the light out, purposely leaving me in complete darkness.

"Hey," I say, shooting up in bed to turn on my desk lamp. "I'm reading over here."

Without so much as an apology, she rolls onto her other side and puts her back to me. I imagine the girls in other rooms, talking nonstop, getting to know each other and sharing stories about families and friends from home.

Of course, I know I'm not alone. Ivy is probably enduring her own silent treatment from Zena. That gives me a little comfort, but I still fall asleep praying I get a new roommate soon.

Seven

I knock on Ivy's door ten minutes before class starts. I'm relieved when she opens it. I'm happy to see her freckled face instead of Zena's. We haven't met, and we don't need to. I already know she isn't going to be a friend of mine.

"Hang on," Ivy says, walking away from the door.

I peek inside and see the same comforter I have on my bed. In fact, if I didn't know any better, I'd think I was looking into my own room. She reappears with a small bag on her shoulder.

"What do you have first period?" I ask.

Ivy shuts the door, then grabs the schedule from her bag. "History of Dowling."

"Perfect. We have the same first class. In fact," I say,

leaning over to look at her schedule more closely, "we have all of our classes together."

Ivy looks as relieved as I feel. "How was the first night with Kendall?"

I pause. "Quiet."

"Same here. It's like living alone," Ivy says.

I don't tell her about snooping in Kendall's envelope and how, in the middle of the night, I had to silently fix her crumpled papers in total darkness.

I don't tell her that I woke up more homesick than I've ever been in my life. That if I could figure out a way to do it without disappointing my parents, I'd split and never look back.

When we walk into history, the room is already half full. Of course, Kendall and Zena aren't there. Kendall is all about making a big entrance, and I assume Zena is probably the same.

Dru is in the front row, toes barely touching the ground. I smile at her and wave, then sit a couple of chairs behind her. Ivy takes the seat next to me.

"Do you know anyone?" I ask Ivy, hoping she might have made friends at dinner last night.

Ivy scans the room, then nods. "A few."

"I only know Dru, the small girl in the front row. She sits on the other side of me in the dining room."

"She's *eleven*?" Ivy asks, eyes wide.

I shrug. "All Seekers are eleven, right?"

A woman I haven't seen before enters the room. She's way younger and way cooler than the dorm moms. She looks like she's a student. There's no way she could be older than seventeen. Her fitted black skirt stops midthigh, and her bright purple shirt almost hurts my eyes. Her black hair is shoulder length, and there are strips of purple died around her face. In my old school a teacher would probably be fired for wearing a dress that short and having purple highlights.

"Well, *that's* different," Ivy says.

I nod, watching our teacher, mesmerized.

She writes her name on the board. *Lady Jennica Silver*.

She turns and raises her hand. I guess all teachers use that signal to get their class quiet, and it works. Everyone in the class stops talking.

"Good morning. I'm Lady Jennica. We have about five minutes before class starts," she says, her voice deeper and raspier than I expected. "You're going to need a spiral-bound notebook and a pencil. You'll be taking a lot of notes today."

Everyone begins digging in their bags for supplies.

I open my spiral and write *History* on the top in perfect cursive. Being a great student has always come easily for me. I'm the nerd who likes school, who always gets her projects turned in early, who's always the teacher's pet. The fact that I don't have a social life makes it easier to be a good student.

Lady Jennica whispers something inaudible, and a PowerPoint suddenly shines on the screen behind her.

She looks at her watch, then snaps her fingers, and the lights dim.

It's like she's a real-life remote.

"Let's get started, shall we?" Lady Jennica asks.

I look at the door, wondering if Kendall is going to be a no-show. That doesn't sound like her. She likes arriving just as the bell rings, but not exactly late.

As if on cue, the door opens and the darkened room floods with light from the hallway.

Zena enters the room first, arms wrapped around a binder in front of her chest. "Sorry, Jennica," she says.

"*Lady* Jennica," the teacher corrects sternly.

"Right," Zena answers, tapping a finger to the side of her head. "*Lady* Jennica."

Zena walks into the room, not embarrassed about her

late arrival. Following close behind her is Kendall, familiar confident smile on her face. My stomach turns at the sight of her.

With Zena in her back pocket, any chance of Dowling leveling the playing field between me and Kendall is gone. Just like my chances of starting over.

Gone.

Gone.

Gone.

It turns out Personal Growth is a time when students are required to research their lineage at Dowling. Most of the girls in our class already know their lineage, but I know almost nothing. Unlike everyone else, who can recite their family tree from memory, I have two pieces of information that constitute the entirety of my knowledge.

1. I have a great-great-grandmother who attended Dowling, named Elsa Whittier Simon.
2. She was a legendary hedge witch.

It's no surprise, then, that I'm the only girl in the library that afternoon. Even Ivy has more information than I do.

The library is lined with elaborate display cases. Everything from books, to stones, to clothes are displayed. I set my books down and walk the perimeter of the library, which seems even bigger with only me in it. I look for anything that might have Elsa Whittier Simon on it, but case after case, there's nothing. I don't know the names of any of the witches in Ivy's family or even Kendall's, so the names on the items have little meaning.

Until I reach a case holding a blood-red ruby necklace. Inscribed on the gold plate in front of it is: *Family necklace, last worn by High Priestess Dannabelle Grimm, 1850.* At the sight of her name, I recall her picture outside the GC. Her eyes were so lifelike, I felt like she could really see me. I can't help but wish my lineage was linked to hers in some way. There's something exciting about Dannabelle that intrigues me. Being a High Priestess beats the warts off digging in the dirt and manipulating herbs as a hedge witch.

The squeaking of the oversize library doors makes my heart stop. I turn to see a custodian entering the room. I can't imagine what she's cleaning. By the looks of things, I'm the only one who's been in the room all day. I smile awkwardly, and the custodian looks away.

I walk away from the display cases and back to my seat. I pull the teacher's research guidelines from my binder and look at the resources I'm supposed to use.

With no online catalog, I am forced to roam the room, looking for the first book on my research list. I check the aisle to make sure I'm in the right place.

I look at every book in the aisle twice, and I'm about to give up when I see a book is out of place, sitting on the floor in the center of the aisle. I look around to see who might have placed the book there, but I'm alone. I look at the custodian and see her mindlessly feather dusting the items inside one of the cases.

There's no one else in the room.

How did that book get on the floor when I'm the only one in the aisle?

My feet are concreted in place. Nothing makes sense. This must be what crazy people feel like.

I pick up the book and read the cover. *History of Hedge Witches.*

It feels like someone's put ice in my veins when I read the title over and over and over.

I stifle the urge to grab my books and run from the room. Instead I take the book and sit down at the desk.

I watch the custodian as she dusts the items in the case. She is haphazard at best and has to catch an item before it falls over.

When a phone rings loudly, I jump in my seat. My heart starts beating again when I see the custodian dig a cell phone out of her pocket. She answers it quietly, then looks at me. Apparently wanting more privacy, she walks out the door, leaving her cleaning cart and the open case behind her.

I sit in my seat for a few minutes, waiting for her to return.

Curious to see the items in the case without the glass barrier, I quietly walk to the case, watching the door for any sign of the custodian's return. On the top shelf is a book that looks like a really big Bible. The gold rectangle in front of it reads, *Book of Shadows Belonging to High Priestess Sarah Goode*. I think of Dru and wonder if this is her ancestor.

On the second shelf is something that looks like the necklace our ID badge is attached to. In history we learned that the necklace is actually an amulet, a happiness amulet. The necklace in the case is much bigger and much fancier. Instead of being made of stones, it has a mixture of stones and gems, each one different from the other.

Hanging from the center of the necklace is a triangular turquoise stone.

I look at the door and think maybe the custodian isn't coming back.

What would happen if I touched it?

The gold plate in front of the necklace reads, *Amulet Belonging to High Priestess Saffra Warnsly.*

Is this *the* Saffra we keep hearing about?

I reach in, looking over my shoulder, listening for the custodian.

I take the necklace in my hand, surprised by how heavy and cold it is.

The clicking of the door stops my breathing, and I watch the door open. I don't have time to put the necklace back in the same position without being caught.

The door opens even more.

Do something, Hallie!

I look at the shelf and shove a pair of shoes into the necklace's place, then toss the gold plate for the amulet behind the book.

The door is halfway open, and I'm standing frozen in front of the open case. Amulet in my hand.

The custodian enters the room, head down, focused

on her phone. I know she's just a footstep away from seeing me.

I'm totally busted. She's going to notice. How could she not notice?

Dropping the necklace into my pocket, I half-run to the nearest bookcase and pretend I'm looking for something.

I may be new to Dowling, but I'm pretty sure I'm breaking all kinds of rules. Snooping, sneaking, stealing. The custodian isn't much better. I'm guessing the headmistress would frown upon her leaving Dowling's most treasured artifacts unprotected like that.

I peek through the bookshelves and watch her close the case, then lock it, phone still pressed to her ear. She looks at my empty desk, then pushes her cart through the door.

Leaving me all alone in the library with a high priestess's amulet in my pocket.

Eight

I speed-walk to the cabinet, holding my breath in the hopes the glass case isn't locked. That by some miracle it's still open and I can return the amulet undetected. I tug at the glass door gently, then a little more roughly. Peering into the glass, I see the thick metal latch that secures the door firmly in place. I'm in *So. Much. Trouble.*

I pull at every single cabinet, on the off chance the custodian left something unlocked. But everything is locked up tight. Maybe I should put the amulet on the librarian's desk. I walk to the wooden counter in the center of the room and find a note.

The Dowling library works on an honor system. If you check out a book, please write your name, the book title, and the date you took it on the form next to this letter. Mark the date when you return it. Because we operate on the honor system, we do not have a librarian. If you need assistance locating an item in the library, please see your instructor or Headmistress Fallon.

Right. I can see it now.

"Headmistress, I'm wondering if you can help me. See, I accidentally stole Saffra's amulet, and now I'd like to return it. Want to help me out?"

Never. Not in a million years.

Just thinking about it makes me want to jump right out the window. That'd be easier to explain than why I have Saffra's amulet.

The only person I trust is Ivy, and she won't be able to help. I bet Heather could open the case, but I don't think she'd keep my criminal activity a secret.

My mind races through the consequences of stealing. Expulsion of me and future generations is a real possibility. Dad would be so upset with me. I can't let that happen.

Think, Hallie. Think.

I can look for the custodian and sneak the key from her pocket. I nearly laugh out loud at the image of me sneaking around a school for witches trying to pickpocket the custodian's keys. My strengths lie in academics, not reconnaissance.

I can hide it somewhere in the library and try to return it the next time the custodian cleans the cases. But what am I going to do? Live in the library until that happens? What if she only cleans the cases once a year?

I can tell a teacher, maybe Lady Jennica. I think about her purple hair and killer clothes. She may be cool, but she's still a teacher. She'd have to tell the headmistress.

Maybe I should leave the necklace on the checkout desk. Surely someone would see it and put it back. But what if someone else takes it? Someone who really shouldn't have it, like Kendall? And what if the custodian gets in trouble? She may not be the most thorough worker in the building, but I don't want to be the reason anyone gets in trouble.

I hurry back to my seat and grab my things from the table. I check to make sure there's absolutely no trace of me being there. I put my hand in my pocket over the amulet to keep it from being seen through my pants. It's cold and bulky, a reminder that it isn't mine. That it belonged to someone way more powerful than I'll ever be.

What have I done? I've been here for only twenty-four hours, and I've already jumped into the dark side with both feet.

I don't let myself think about what's going to happen to me for taking the amulet, what wretched forces of evil the amulet's real owner will throw down on me.

I don't think about that.

I don't think about anything.

I power walk out of the library like I'm being chased by Saffra herself on a runaway broom, and race to find Ivy.

I rap my knuckles on Ivy's door.

Knock. Knock. Knock.

I tap my foot, desperate for Ivy to answer.

Knock. Knock. Knock. Louder this time.

The door finally opens, but instead of Ivy I'm face-to-face with Zena.

"Where's the fire, dork?" she asks.

Over her shoulder I see Kendall on Zena's bed, smirking at me.

"Is Ivy here?" I ask.

"No." Zena begins to close the door, and I stop it with my hand.

"Do you know where she is?"

Zena sighs, hand on her hip, totally irritated with me. "She's in the lobby studying."

Before I can thank her, she slams the door in my face. I'm too panicked to be upset, and walk as fast as I can to the lobby. Ivy is sitting cross-legged on one of the oversize leather couches, a spiral in her lap and a textbook open next to her. Thankfully, no one else is sitting with her.

I drop down beside her and put my hand on her spiral.

"Need something?" she asks, half-smiling. When she sees my face, she gets serious. "What's wrong?"

I look around the open room and see clusters of girls talking and studying, their voices echoing in the large space. "We can't talk here." I start grabbing her things while she watches me. "Let's go to my room."

She puts an arm on my leg to stop my frenetic activity. "First of all, relax."

I notice some girls watching us and realize I'm drawing more attention than I want by acting like a crazed maniac.

"Second, let me have my things so I can pack them up."

I hand her the items I took from her and let her pack, frustrated when she doesn't do so as quickly as I'd like.

"Come on," I whisper, then stand from the couch and

begin race-walking to my room. I look over my shoulder and see her walking at a normal pace. *A normal pace!* Like there's no emergency. Can't she tell by looking at me that something has gone horribly wrong?

When she finally gets to my room, I lock the dead bolt, then sit on my bed and motion for her to do the same.

"Are you okay?" Ivy asks, eyebrows drawn close together in worry. "Because you look awful."

"Well, that's exactly how I feel. Awful."

I pull the amulet from my pocket and drop it onto the bed between us.

She looks at it blankly. "What's that?"

"An amulet," I tell her. "Like ours but way more important."

"Your grandmother's?" she asks.

I shake my head so fast, I give myself a little headache.

"So whose is it, Hallie?" The tone in her voice tells me she's catching on, that she knows I'm not supposed to have this amulet.

I'm afraid to say it out loud. Afraid to trust anyone with the truth. Even Ivy.

"Hallie," she says, sounding way more like my mother than my friend. "What are you doing with this amulet?"

I hold it, nervously tracing the carvings in the stone and avoiding Ivy's eyes. I don't want to tell her. But I have to tell someone. No way I can keep this a secret.

Without raising my eyes, I tell her the whole story. I tell her about the book on the ground, about the custodian leaving the library, about me picking up the amulet, and about me walking out with it.

When I finish talking, I force myself to look at her.

Ivy's face is serious but not panicked, and that alone helps me relax. Just telling her makes me breathe easier. Ivy's smart. She'll know what to do.

"Well, that's got to be some kind of record for this place." She smiles big, then giggles. "Think anyone's stolen an artifact from the Dowling display cases on their first day before?"

I slap at her playfully. "Not funny. Not even close to funny."

"Seriously. What were you thinking?"

"I was just curious. I didn't think the custodian would be back so soon. I could still hear her talking on the telephone, for crying out loud. When she walked back in, I panicked. I got as far away from those cabinets as quickly as I could."

"Whose amulet is it? Do you know?"

A war battles inside my head.

Tell her. Don't tell her.

Tell her. Don't tell her.

"I promise I won't freak out." Ivy holds up two Girl Scout fingers. "Promise."

"If you tell anyone, I'll—"

"Relax, already. I don't rat my friends out."

Something in her eyes reaches me. I know I can trust her.

"Saffra Warnsly." My words are barely a whisper.

"Saffra? *The* Saffra Warnsly!" Ivy is on her feet, looking at the amulet like it's cursed.

I stare back at my only friend, words lost.

"Oh, Hallie. You've really done it now."

"What happened to you not panicking? You're panicking!" I remind her, my voice rising an octave.

"Well, I didn't think you'd have *Saffra's* amulet. Do you even know who Saffra is?"

I shrug, embarrassed to admit my own ignorance. Not knowing the answer to every question is new territory for me, and I don't like it.

"Saffra Warnsly was the first High Priestess of the

Dowling Coven. She was one of many witches tried in the Salem Witch Trials. She is the goddess we pray to, for Sa—" She's silent just a millisecond. "For heaven's sake. Haven't you noticed how often we say her name?"

I nod, my face hotter than a blazing campfire. "I didn't know who she was." And I really wish I didn't know now.

"Well, the solution is simple. You have to get it back in the case. Immediately."

I keep looking at her, my mind a total blank. "How do I do that?"

Ivy sits in my desk chair and looks out the window. "We have to get the custodian's key somehow. This place probably has a dozen custodians, and they're all assigned specific areas to clean. Do you remember what she looks like?"

I close my eyes, trying to visualize the woman. "Dark hair in a ponytail. Kind of short, just a little taller than me."

"Think, Hallie. Did you see her name on her uniform?"

I shake my head. "I was never that close to her. But she did have a mole on her face. I could see that from the desk I was working at. It was on her right cheek, close to her eye."

"Good. Good." Ivy taps her fingernails on the desk in thought.

"If we figure out who she is, maybe we can get the key from her," I say. "They keep all their keys on a huge ring, right? I can make up some lie about needing something in a classroom. Say I left my things in there. But instead I'll go back to the library and put the amulet back where it belongs."

"Good. Good," Ivy repeats. "That's a real good plan."

"What do I do with it until then?"

Ivy stares at the amulet on my bed, like she might get hexed just for being in the same room. "I have no idea. You can't trust Kendall."

I laugh out loud. "Not at all."

"So you can't leave it in your room," she says. "And you're sure not keeping it in *my* room."

"Maybe we could tell Miss A?" I offer. "She's so nice and seems totally understanding. I bet she's seen this kind of thing happen before. She's been a dorm mom forever, right?"

"Are you nuts?" Ivy asks. "You want to tell one of the most important people in this building that you *accidentally* stole Saffra's amulet? Do you know how crazy that would be? It'd be a death sentence. They'd probably send you home."

Home? That sounds like a really good idea at the

moment. Ivy must read the thoughts in my head, because she snaps her fingers in front of my face. "Don't even think about leaving me here alone."

In spite of the mess I'm in, the fact that Ivy wants me here makes me feel infinitely better. And I'd rather choke on a frog than give Kendall the satisfaction of telling me I couldn't cut it at Dowling.

"And what would this do to your parents? To your family? Are you really prepared to have your entire family expelled from Dowling?"

A sick feeling ping-pongs in my stomach like a Mexican jumping bean.

"So if I can't tell Kendall, and I can't tell Miss A, what do I do with this?" I point at the amulet.

"You're going to have to wear it under your shirt."

"*Wear* it? Are you crazy? No way. That can't be the only option. Besides, it's huge. People will see it through my shirt."

Ivy nods in agreement. "You're going to have to wear the sweater vest. It's bulky enough to hide it."

"A sweater vest? In *September*? It's close to a hundred degrees outside right now."

"You stole Saffra's amulet, and you're worried about being hot? Really?"

I sigh, knowing she's right and wishing like crazy I'd just skipped the library altogether today. I grab the amulet from the bed and carefully drape it around my neck. I slip it under my shirt and grab a sweater vest from the dresser before taking off my glasses. "I'm going to be the only person in the building wearing a sweater vest."

"Stop complaining."

I pull it over my head and put my glasses back on.

Ivy adjusts the vest, then fixes my collar. She stands back to look at me. "Perfect. Can't see a thing."

I cross my arms over my chest. "Fine. I'll wear it. But I'm not going to like it."

Nine

"What are you wearing?" Kendall asks when she opens the door to our room. Her tone is ridicule mixed with contempt. The amulet, warm against my skin as it hides beneath the sweater, gives me comfort. If I can forget I'm wearing a stolen amulet right here, right now, I almost feel confident.

I'm three steps away from Kendall, headed to a Seeker meeting with Miss A. I decide to ignore her question and try to match her tone. "You're going the wrong way. Our meeting with Miss A starts in five minutes."

Kendall motions to my outfit. "You've got enough going on. Let me worry about my schedule."

I bite back the words fighting to be set free.

I'm done trying to help you.

You can't just blow off Miss A the way you blew off our other teachers.

Hey, can you see Saffra's amulet under this?

I step out into the hall and see Dru a couple of doors down, talking to someone I don't know. She must feel me watching her, because she turns suddenly, then smiles and waves me over.

"Hi, Hallie," she says. "What'd you think of the first day?"

I put my hand on my chest, feel the security of the amulet. Just touching it, though, reminds me how much trouble I'll be in when they realize it's missing. "Crazy."

"If you ask me," the other girl says, "this is pretty lame. I thought we were going to learn how to be witches, not just go to regular classes and research our ancestry."

I look at the name on her badge. Josephina Carrier.

"I go by Jo. No one—not even my mother—calls me Josephina."

I give her a thumbs-up. "Jo. Got it."

"Jo's my roommate," Dru says.

The two are a totally mismatched pair. Dru reminds me of a fairy, and Jo reminds me of a linebacker. Jo's at least twice Dru's size and looks like she hasn't smiled in long, long time. Maybe never. Where Dru is dark skinned,

Jo is as pale a person as I've ever seen. Her blond hair is thin and wispy, and overgrown bangs hang in front of her face. It's a stark difference from Dru's happy curls that bounce with every step.

Dru will be good for Jo. Maybe she'll lighten her up a little.

Ivy calls to me from her doorway. "Wait for me!"

I nod in answer.

"Do you know where the Seeker Sanctum is?" I ask Dru. "It wasn't on our map."

She shrugs happily. Again I wish I had her personality. I bet nothing bothers her. I wonder how she'd handle having Saffra's stolen amulet hiding beneath her clothes.

"I know where it is," Ivy says when she walks up. "It's one of the specialty rooms downstairs." Downstairs? I hope it isn't in the basement. I shiver at the thought.

We all start moving in that direction and follow Ivy down the narrow staircase. After a turn to the right, we come to a room similar to the GC but much smaller. Rows of chairs sit in a half-circle around a small triangular platform. Candles light the room, and it's almost full. The tension in my body releases. This room doesn't feel like a creepy basement at all.

Miss A greets us as we enter. "C'mon on in, girls. Nothing to be afraid of."

She's wearing a wild print dress that almost looks like a nightgown. Her hair is characteristically out of control, her curls a mixture of gray and blond and maybe a hint of red. Looks like someone's been experimenting with the hair dye. She really should just pick a color and stick with it. I look for the curl with eyes that I saw when Ivy fainted, but nothing's there. I must have been in shock.

Miss A shoves a loose curl off her face. "Darn hair has a mind of its own."

At the mention of her hair, I look at her closely, wondering if she can read my thoughts the way the headmistress can. But Miss A is already welcoming other girls, her hair forgotten.

Ivy points to some empty seats on the far side of the room. "Let's go over there."

The four of us sit down, and Dru immediately starts talking to the girls around us. I don't know how, but she seems to know and like everyone. And it's obvious everyone likes her. It's hard not to.

Jo, on the other hand, is sulking in her seat. "This better be more exciting than last night."

"What were you expecting? A full-blown magic show?" Ivy asks.

"Something more than an out-of-control candle."

Miss A takes the stage, and I glance around the room as it turns quiet. Kendall and Zena are noticeably absent. Frustration has me gritting my teeth. I don't know why I care. She's not my responsibility.

Miss A opens her mouth to speak, then stops when Kendall and Zena enter the room. "Welcome, girls. There are two seats right here in the front." She waves them over, and I look at the seats she's referring to. I can't help but giggle when I see they aren't together. When Zena and Kendall glare at the open seats and their distance from one another, Miss A hurries them along.

"Quick like a fox, girls," she says with three quick claps of her hands. "If sitting together is important, you'll need to arrive early."

Ivy has her hand over her mouth, laughing silently.

"Score one for Miss A," I whisper.

Once the two are seated, Miss A begins. "Welcome, my Seekers. I am so thrilled to be part of your first year at Dowling. I know you must have a lot of questions, and I'll answer them all, but first I want to talk to you about the hierarchy at Dowling. Please take the paper from under your chair and follow along."

I look under my chair and grab the paper.

"Were these here earlier? I don't remember seeing them." Ivy looks at me, eyes narrowed.

I shake my head. "They weren't here. I'd have noticed."

Ivy turns to Jo. "There's your magic. Happy?"

Jo doesn't respond, just looks at the paper in complete boredom.

"Let's start at the top, shall we?" Miss A says. I follow along as she reads the hierarchy to us.

DOWLING COVEN HIERARCHY			
YEAR	TITLE	TOOL	DESCRIPTION OF LEVEL
1	Seeker	Happiness Amulet & Book of Shadows	A person committed to studying the practices of witchcraft for a year and a day. Students must successfully learn cantrips (beginner spells).
2	Crafter	Crystal	Upon the successful completion of the second year and a day of study required of a Crafter, members of the coven evaluate a student witch. This evaluation is done to determine if the student should be invited to become a full member of the coven as a fourth circle witch or asked to leave.

The XYZs of Being Wicked ...·*·*·*··.·*·*·.

YEAR	TITLE	TOOL	DESCRIPTION OF LEVEL
3	Fourth Circle	Robe & Cauldron	After an initiation ceremony, the student witch becomes a fourth circle witch, meaning she is considered a witch in the eyes of the coven. The witch is given her official robe.
4	Third Circle	Wand	At the end of a year and a day of work in the fourth circle, the witch is evaluated by second circle witches. If considered successful in her work over the past year, she is elevated to a third circle witch.
5	Second Circle	Pendulum	A third circle witch spends at least another year, sometimes up to two years, studying to become a second circle witch. When this degree of evaluation is reached, she takes on the responsibilities of being a teacher in the coven and may use the title "Lady" or "Lord" within the circle to show her new status.
6	First Circle	Athame	Witches who successfully reach the first circle are eligible to become the High Priestess because the leadership responsibilities have been learned. Candidates for High Priestess must undergo special training and then test to demonstrate their leadership capabilities and devotion to the coven.

"I know what you're thinking," Miss A says when she's finished reading aloud. "There's a lot of work ahead. And you're right. There is. But I promise it will be fun. You may have noticed in the GC how students sit by rows. Well, this is how we determine who sits where. The first circle witches are on the first row because they are our most powerful witches. One of them may even be our next High Priestess."

I wonder how High Priestesses are chosen. Do they have to take a test? Is there an election?

Miss A clasps her hands in front of her chest. "Let's move on. Now, once a year Dowling has a social. A coed social."

Excited giggling and talking consumes the room. Even Ivy's eyes are sparkling. I may be the only girl in the room who really doesn't care about boys. Okay, so that's not entirely true. I always had a crush on Jasper Williams back home, but the only girl he ever noticed was Kendall. Something she was always happy to remind me of.

In my experience, every time a girl likes a boy, she acts stupid and ignores her friends. I just don't think boys are worth all the drama.

"Quiet down, ladies," Miss A says, hand held above her head.

I wonder if we have to go. Maybe I can stay behind and learn how to become more . . . I don't know . . . witchy. Even a night of cleaning my dorm room sounds better than a social.

When the room grows quiet, Miss A continues. Her face is lit with excitement, and the smile on her face is contagious. If she's this excited about it, maybe it's better than I thought.

"The dance is held at Riley Academy, Dowling's brother school."

Everyone in the room looks as surprised as me. Everyone except Kendall. I wonder if she knew about Riley. She always had a knack for knowing things before everyone else.

Miss A continues. "Riley Academy is about twenty minutes away. Every year, they host the coed social, which is basically just a dance. They always do a really nice job."

Hands shoot up into the air. Miss A answers the questions, taking her time to make sure everyone knows what to expect.

"Yes, you may wear your own clothes. Uniforms are not required."

"No, you may not stay here. Attendance is mandatory."

"No, you may not wear makeup."

I think about the handful of outfits I brought from home. I'm not sure any of them are dance-worthy, but I remind myself I don't care anyway. I'm only going because I have to. I couldn't care less about boys.

Couldn't. Care. Less.

"Before we dismiss, does anyone have other questions?" Miss A asks, eyes hopeful.

Kendall's hand shoots up first. "Can we switch rooms?"

Miss A looks at me, her face sad, then looks back at Kendall. "I'm sorry, Kendall. We don't allow room switching at the Seeker level. If you elevate to the Crafter level, then you may choose your roommate."

I can see the hope drain from Kendall like air from a popped balloon. I'm secretly satisfied we can't change rooms, if only to keep Kendall from getting her way.

Jo raises her hand.

"Yes, Jo?" Miss A asks.

"When are we going to learn some magic? I mean, isn't that why we came here?"

Miss A smiles, the picture of patience. "When your instructors feel that you are ready, and not a second before."

Several other questions are asked, but I tune them out.

Twenty-four hours ago my life was normal. No magic, no rituals, no hierarchy I had to somehow master.

Despite the doubt dancing in my stomach, I force myself to quiet my nerves. This is my reality. My new life. And I, Hallie Simon, will be the best darn witch Dowling has ever seen.

Ten

Ivy and I are walking to class the next morning when we see Miss A.

With bright orange hair.

I remember my thoughts from last night. How I thought she should choose a color and stick with it.

"Morning, girls! Watcha think?" she asks, fluffing her freshly dyed hair.

Ivy speaks first. "Bold, just like you. It's perfect!"

I stare at Miss A, stunned. "Yeah, bold."

Miss A smiles. "You girls are so sweet. There could be worms in my hair, and you wouldn't say anything. See you two later."

Ivy starts walking, but I'm cemented to the ground. I thought about Miss A's hair needing to be dyed last night.

And she dyed it. Last night. Is it some sort of coincidence? Or did I put some unknown witchy spell on her?

I speed-walk to catch up with Miss A, abandoning a confused Ivy in the hallway.

"Miss A," I call to her.

She turns around, a huge smile on her face. It's so contagious, I have to smile back.

"What's up, buttercup?" she asks cheerfully.

I look at my feet, then back at my dorm mother. "I was just wondering why you decided to dye your hair last night."

She props her hands on her waist. "Well, I guess I don't know. I just thought it was time to pick a color and stick with it."

Pick a color and stick with it. Are those the exact same words I thought yesterday? They are. I know they are!

Miss A's face shifts to a look of concern. "Something bothering you, sugar? You can trust me with anything. Whatever you tell me goes in the vault."

She pretends she's locking her mouth and throwing away the key. If I didn't know how powerful she actually was, she'd be really hard to take seriously.

I consider telling her about the amulet, and my hand

goes to my chest. I can't tell her. There's no way I can tell her.

Fake smile on my face, I shake my head. "Umm. Well . . . your hair really looks great."

She pulls me to her for a quick, smushy hug. "Thanks, doll. You better get to class. Lady Jennica doesn't like it when students are late."

In the time it takes me to walk back to where Ivy is standing impatiently, I decide not to tell Ivy what I thought last night. It *has* to be a coincidence. But how can I know for sure? Maybe I should try it out. Just a little.

As we walk into Lady Jennica's class, I ask Ivy, "Do you always wear your hair in braids?"

"Always," she answers. "My hair is supercurly, and it's out of control if I don't do the braid thing."

Wear your hair down, Ivy. Try something new.

"Ever think about wearing it down? You know, just let it all hang out?" I continue.

She shakes her head. "Not a chance. It's crazy curly and impossible to control. Serious."

"I bet it's pretty."

"You'd lose that bet."

Lady Jennica walks in, wearing a solid black dress

with heels high enough to make her nose bleed. I wonder if becoming a second, third, or fourth circle witch makes you incredibly beautiful. The older the girls at Dowling, the more stunning they seem to be. And Lady Jennica is no exception. Compared to the Seekers in her class, she is runway-model material.

With a twirl of her hand, the door closes and the lights dim.

Just as the projector comes to life, Kendall and Zena enter the room. When Lady Jennica looks at the clock above the door, I follow her eyes. The two are a full minute late.

Once they're seated, Lady Jennica raises her hand slowly, and the lights become brighter.

She sits on the edge of her huge wooden desk, crosses her legs, and pointedly looks at the latecomers.

"Perhaps this is the time to discuss my feelings on tardiness," she says. It sounds like she's speaking to the entire class of eighteen girls, but she's looking only at Kendall and Zena.

"Every second of every minute in this room counts. Miss Fallon, I assume you think you already know more about Dowling than the rest of the girls. Because you've been here so long, I suspect you are correct in that assumption."

I'm dying to see Zena's face, but all I can see is her ramrod-stiff back. Tense, maybe?

"However, that does not excuse you from my class, or any other class. When you arrive late, you are disrespecting not only me but also your Dowling sisters who arrived on time. Kendall and Zena, we've had two classes, and you've been late to both of them. Going forward, I will not allow you to enter the room after nine o'clock. If you are not in the room and in your seat by that time, you will be counted absent and I will discuss the issue with your parents."

I sit on my hands to keep from clapping, and it's clear everyone in the room feels exactly the same way I do—victorious. Like there really might be equality inside the Dowling walls after all.

"You will not receive special treatment, Zena. There are others in this room whose heritage would demand such treatment, yet they arrive prepared, respectful, and on time."

Zena's head turns, and she looks to see who could possibly be more important than her.

Lady Jennica walks to my desk. "Have you met Hallie Simon?"

Zena rolls her eyes, then turns back around and puts her back to me. "Hallie's the descendent of Dowling's most powerful hedge witch. Hedge witches can heal the sickest of the sick and can restore harmony to any situation. They're extraordinarily important. Hallie and her hedge witch ancestry add a great deal of power to Dowling. But she will not receive special treatment."

As Zena shoots me a murderous glare, Lady Jennica pats my shoulder with a wink before returning to the front of the room. "All of you come with special gifts. Your *karama*. But none of you will receive special favors or treatment, regardless of how flashy your gifts are. Over the next several weeks you'll be discovering what those gifts are. This is part of the reason you're required to conduct ancestry research so early in the year. So that you know your past and can share that with your classmates. Trust me, girls. You may be powerful on your own, but you're an unbreakable force when you work together."

Before I shower the following morning, I triple-check to make sure the door is locked, then carefully put the amulet under my towel. It'd be really weird for Kendall to come into the bathroom while I'm showering, but I don't want to leave anything to chance. *No one* can know about the amulet besides Ivy.

When I step out of the bathroom, I'm fully dressed, including the sweater vest.

Kendall passes me with a dramatic eye roll. "Loser," she mutters under her breath.

For once her put-downs don't bother me. After seeing her and Zena put in their places yesterday, I have renewed hope about being here. If Zena won't get special treatment, then neither will Kendall. And that means I have a chance of being normal, maybe even popular.

The clock on my desk reads eight fifteen. I promised to meet Ivy in the dining room at eight twenty. Breakfast is open seating, so we get to sit together.

I put on my black loafers and pull my hair back with a headband. It's my normal, no-fuss look. The whole no-makeup rule is really working in my favor. My face is flawless, while other girls are already battling pimples because of the makeup they used to wear. I know that rule changes next year, but until then I'm just like everyone else.

I add my glasses, making me officially ready for the day.

Grabbing my bag, I head out the door without a good-bye to my roommate. It feels empowering somehow, to do that. Like I'm the one beating her for a change.

I put my hand on my chest, making sure the amulet is still with me. I'm hoping to see the custodian from the library in the dining room this morning. I haven't seen her once since that first night. And until I find her, I can't borrow her key.

The dining room is alive with students and teachers, some eating, some talking, some studying. I search the room for Ivy but don't see her. Dru waves to me, and I wave back. I get in line, grab a plate, and cover it with fruit, eggs, and a muffin. I tuck a pint of orange juice under my arm and walk out of the food line.

Before I reach the table, my eyes are drawn to the dining room door. My feet stop moving and my mouth drops open.

Walking through the door at that very moment is Ivy, hair down.

Eleven

I stare . . . stunned, speechless, and scared.

I thought it.

Then *it* happened.

Ivy left her hair down.

She pulls at it self-consciously, her useless attempt to flatten the thick curls around her face. She looks less like a farm girl and more like a Disney character. With her hair down her green eyes seem greener, and each freckle more visible.

Ivy sees me and walks to our table, her feet moving fast to avoid the eyes watching her. It's like a new student has arrived. A new student from Mars.

Dru's the first to speak. "Wow! Look at your hair."

Ivy shakes her head, then yanks at the ponytail holders around her wrist. "I should put it up."

"No, no," I tell her. "Leave it down. It's really pretty."

"It's pretty now," she mutters.

We sit down across from Dru and Jo.

When Jo finally looks up from her plate piled high with bacon, she gives Ivy a *What the hey* look. She shakes her head, then turns back to her bacon.

"What made you decide to leave your hair down?" I ask her.

Ivy shrugs, but that answer isn't good enough for me. I *have* to know.

"Yesterday you said you never put your hair down," I remind her.

She looks at me, confused. "I did, didn't I?"

"Yep." I focus on getting the food from my plate to my mouth. Otherwise I might scream and jump and tell her what I thought yesterday.

"Huh," she says absently, then grabs a mini muffin from my plate.

"It looks great," I tell her. And it really does. She was right—her hair is curly, but it's far from out of control.

I think back to yesterday, and how I specifically thought about Ivy leaving her hair down. I was testing myself to see if I could control her thoughts. Never in a bazillion years did I think I could. But looking at her now, it's hard to pretend yesterday didn't happen.

First Miss A's hair, now Ivy's. Maybe I can only control people's hair. That'd be a weird—and totally useless— gift. Perfect. If that's it, if that's my power, I'm leaving. What kind of a witch would that be? I'd never hear the end of it from Kendall. Of course, it *would* be nice to make Kendall's hair a righteous mess.

Jo pops another slice of bacon into her mouth. I'm not normally bothered by people eating meat, but for some reason the smell of her bacon is more than I can stomach today.

"Our Elements of Witchcraft class is going to be good today. I heard someone say we're supposed to begin exploring our gifts," Dru says.

Mouth full, Jo mumbles, "About time."

I stifle an eye roll. *This is only our third day.*

"I know it's only our third day, but still. I was expecting more." Jo puts her hand over her mouth to cover a small burp. The smell of burped bacon hits my nose, and my mouth waters, a warning sign I'm about to be sick.

Please throw that bacon away before I puke.

Ivy looks at the food line like she wants to get something to eat, but stays seated.

"Anyone want my bacon? I'm full." Jo pushes the plate forward, but no one takes it. Not even Ivy, who looks so hungry, she could eat an entire hog.

"I'll just throw it away, then."

My hand freezes on its way to my mouth. Banana in hand, I stare at Jo.

"Why would you throw bacon away?"

Jo shrugs. "Thought that would make you happy, little miss vegetarian."

My heart bangs in my chest like a basketball, and I bounce my legs nervously.

First she copies my thoughts about it being our third day, and then the bacon.

Can *everyone* hear my thoughts? How do they know what I'm thinking?

Jo pushes out her chair so forcefully, it falls back, but before it can hit the ground, it pops back up.

"That was close," Miss A says, walking by. A tiny curl springs loose and moves freely above her head before she swipes it down. She's dressed like she's headed to a Cinco de Mayo party, not witch school.

"Nice hair, Red!" Miss A gives Ivy a thumbs-up, then marches on in her oversize Mexican dress and bright red flats. The only thing missing is an oversize sombrero.

"See?" My voice squeaks. "Everyone likes it."

"No offense, but Miss A isn't exactly my go-to fashion guru." Ivy takes a small bunch of grapes from my plate, but I don't mind.

I'm too nervous or anxious or scared to do much more than breathe.

I put my hand to my stomach, let the weight of the amulet calm me, and clear my mind so I can make it through the day. Something tells me it's going to be wicked.

Lady Rose sits on her stool and waits for the class to quiet down. Unlike Lady Jennica, this teacher is closer to my mom's age. Like my mom, I think she probably knows the answers to all my questions.

She's always dressed in black and wears a bright emerald necklace. Her blond hair is short but fashionable. It always looks like she just woke up and ran her fingers through it, but it's somehow impossibly perfect. Her voice is warm and reassuring—exactly what I need today.

The elements classroom is set up like a science lab and always smells of the incense Lady Rose burns on her desk. Normally it's my favorite room.

But not today.

Today the room is buzzing with excited voices, everyone anxious to learn what their gift is.

A chorus of shushing is followed by silence.

"Well, I guess you've all heard that today is the beginning of gift exploration."

The room nods in unison.

"I should warn you that this is a process. It's a lot more complicated than just pulling a name from a hat. Some of you might already be experiencing your gift. Most of you, though, have not."

She lowers herself from the stool and sends a quick flip of her hand to the ceiling. The room is now dark enough that it's hard to see Ivy sitting next to me.

Lady Rose's voice is soft, smooth, soothing.

"You will learn your first spell today. Its purpose is to open the gift inside you. This spell is only performed once in a witch's life. For you that is today."

I take a deep breath, more afraid than excited. If I already think people can read my mind, what's going to happen after this?

"There's nothing to fear, girls."

There it is again!

Now Lady Rose is reading my mind. Or maybe she isn't. Maybe she says that to everyone.

Another deep breath.

Chill. Out.

"Please listen to the spell as I say it. You will repeat it after me the second time, but this time just listen and think. Think about what the words are invoking in you."

The room is silent. So silent I can hear the electricity buzzing through the dimmed lights.

"Hear us now, the words of the witches,
the secrets we hide in the night.
Our magic is sought,
invoke our power,
in this hour,
bring our gifts to light."

My mind shoots back to the attic, to the Book of Shadows, to the storm I somehow created there.

I've heard this spell.

I've *said* this spell.

What happens if I've already said the spell? Will I be twice as powerful if I say it again? I don't *want* to be twice as powerful. Should I stop the class and tell Lady Rose?

"Seekers, repeat after me."

It's too late to do anything, so I repeat the spell with my hand on the vibrating amulet.

I've been part of Dowling for three days, and I've already said a spell I shouldn't have and stolen a High Priestess's amulet. Way to go, Hallie.

"Breathe in," Lady Rose instructs.

I suck up all the air I can.

"Breathe out," she whispers.

The class exhales, and the lights slowly brighten.

Everyone in the room is looking at each other, eyes never resting on one person too long, like they're afraid of what they might see.

Jo is the first to speak. "That's it?"

Lady Rose giggles in a just-wait-and-see kind of way. "The change isn't instantaneous, Jo. For some of you it could take weeks, even months, to determine your gift."

"So how will we know what our gift is?" Ivy asks.

"Look around," our teacher says. "This is a room built for experimenting. You will journal your experiences. Anything new you feel or sense should be written down. I'll visit with you about your journal daily so that I can guide you. For example, if you feel that you have the power to move objects, we will test that here. I will teach you how to develop your gift in a way that helps others. It is imperative that you remember that. The Dowling coven doesn't tolerate dabbling in black magic."

Kendall and Zena give each other a knowing look. My stomach roils like a ready-for-children witch's brew. That look means trouble. I don't know how or when or where, but trouble is coming. And if history repeats itself, I'm right in the line of fire.

Twelve

I stare at the journal on my lap. With Kendall in the shower this is my chance to write. She's been watching me way too closely since we got to our room after dinner. I managed to ignore her—and the journal—by reading the hedge witch book.

Lady Rose made it clear she expects us to journal every day, even if we aren't experiencing anything new. Kendall wrote in her journal for at least an hour, then put it away with a smug smile and satisfied sigh.

I glance at her book bag, wishing I had the guts to look in her journal. But it feels wrong. I've already broken enough rules at Dowling by accident. I sure don't need to break any on purpose. Lady Rose said some of us already know what our gift is, and I'm sure Kendall and Zena are two of those. They act like they know everything about everyone.

I put my pencil to the clean white paper, but I don't write. If I put it in writing, someone could find it. Kendall could read it. Then where would I be? The last thing I need is her messing with me while I'm trying to figure out my gift.

I decide to go cryptic.

Headmistress.

Miss A's hair.

Ivy's hair.

Bacon.

There. I've journaled.

When Kendall comes out of the bathroom, she glances in my direction, then immediately looks away.

I close the journal and put it into my book bag. "You know, you won't turn to salt if you talk to me."

Kendall acts like she didn't hear me.

"You'll see," I tell her. "You're going to need me one day, and then you'll *have* to talk to me."

This gets a snort from Kendall.

I turn off the lamp and slide under my covers. Hand on the amulet, I whisper, "You're going to need me. You'll see."

*   *   *   *   *   *

Lady Jennica leans against her desk, a small basket in her hand.

"Seekers, today you'll begin research on some of Dowling's most influential High Priestesses."

Excitement pumps the blood through my veins at lightning speed.

Dannabelle.

"The good news is, you won't be doing it alone. You will work with a partner to complete the project."

I immediately look to Ivy, who gives me a thumbs-up. Group projects aren't my favorite thing in the world because I always end up doing all the work. But if I can work with Ivy, I know it'll be fine. Maybe even fun.

"Your assignment is to choose a High Priestess to research. You will work together on all aspects of the research, the report writing, and the creation of a Power-Point to present your information to the class."

The room is humming as girls find friends to partner with. Kendall and Zena are already moving their desks closer together. My hands white-knuckle the edge of my desk. They'd better not pick Dannabelle. She's mine.

"The bad news," says Lady Jennica, pausing until she

knows everyone's listening, "is that you don't get to choose your partner."

My heart skids to a screeching stop. Zena and Kendall pause in their desk arranging.

Lady Jennica shakes the basket in front of her, ignoring the moans from the students. "We'll leave the partnering to fate."

Fate? *That's* what I'm relying on?

I look at Ivy, fingers crossed. She crosses her fingers too as Lady Jennica pulls the first name. "Dru Goode," she says, then walks the basket to Dru. "Pick your partner."

Dru pulls a name I've never heard from the basket. Dru's permanent smile never leaves her face. "Cool."

Lady Jennica repeats the process several more times before she reaches someone I know. "Jo Carrier."

Jo pulls a name from the basket, then smiles in my direction. "Ivy Oliver," she says.

I'm briefly disappointed. I really wanted to be partners with Ivy.

I whip around to look at Ivy, then look at the other girls in the room whose names haven't been called. Kendall and Zena are still partnerless, and so am I.

Lady Jennica calls several more names, then finally

calls mine. "Hallie Simon." She walks the nearly empty basket to my desk. I fumble around for a piece of paper that feels right. One hand on the amulet under my shirt for luck, I pick a piece of paper.

I hold it in my hand and take a deep breath.

"Open it," Lady Jennica says softly, like she knows why I'm hesitating.

I look up at her dark eyes.

"It will be okay," she promises.

Unable to stall another second, I slowly unfold the paper and swallow the panic lodged in my throat. When I speak, I barely recognize my shaky voice. "Kendall Scott."

Kendall turns around slowly. *"What?"*

I match her glare but don't bother answering her.

Lady Jennica calls another name, but I tune out the rest of the process. All I can focus on is the fact that I have to work with Kendall. So much for fate.

"Please move so you're sitting with your partner. I'm handing out a list of High Priestesses you may research and the guidelines for the project. Raise your hand when you know which priestess you'd like to learn more about."

Kendall doesn't move.

Neither does Zena.

A girl walks to the seat in front of Zena and says, "I'm Jessie."

Zena crosses her arms over her chest. I don't know Jessie, but I feel as sorry for her as I do for myself.

"I'm sorry," Ivy mouths as she moves closer to Jo. I'd give *anything* to be partners with Jo. With anyone except Kendall.

When Lady Jennica sees that neither me nor Kendall are moving, she walks to Kendall's desk and puts her hand on her shoulder. "There's a free seat next to your partner. Please take your things and move."

Kendall pauses, then grabs her binder like she wants to throw it across the room. When she sits down next to me, she mutters, "This stinks."

For once I agree with her.

"I've already picked our High Priestess," I tell her, forcing my voice to be confident.

I'm shocked she doesn't argue, so I raise my hand.

Lady Jennica comes by with a clipboard. "That was fast. Who's your High Priestess?"

"Dannabelle Grimm, please."

She smiles. "She's fun. You're going to enjoy your research."

I grin smugly at Kendall. She'll never admit it, but she'll be glad I picked Dannabelle.

"Let's divide the research," Kendall suggests, turning the paper to see the teacher's research guidelines.

"Remember, girls," Lady Jennica says above the voices already working. "You *must* work on this together. You cannot divide and conquer, then combine your efforts at the end. And don't attempt to fool me. I'm a witch, remember? I have gifts you can't even imagine."

The room goes quiet with the reminder that Dowling isn't like other schools.

"We need to work in the library," I say. At the thought of the library, I grab the amulet.

I have to put the amulet back.

"Fine. We can meet during our Personal Growth time."

"Start today?" I ask.

She shakes her head.

"Kendall, I'm not putting this off to the last minute."

She stares back at me, eyes tiny little squints of pure hate.

"You have to work with me. You need me, like it or not."

When the words come out of my mouth, we look at each other strangely. What I just said is almost exactly what I said to Kendall last night. Then I thought it again before I went to sleep. I put my hand on the amulet and thought it.

"Wait a minute," Kendall says. "What did you do?"

I shake my head and stare at the paper on my desk until the letters fade away.

All I can see, all I can think, all I can hear is the whisper of my own voice last night.

You're going to need me.

You'll see.

Thirteen

We have to find the library custodian," I tell Ivy. We're walking to lunch, but I can't eat. I'm focused on getting this amulet back into the library case. Too many weird things have happened already.

"What about lunch?" Ivy asks, following me as I zip past the dining room.

I don't answer, just walk into the library to see if she's there.

But it's empty again.

"Hallie," Ivy says, touching my shoulder gently. "What's going on? You're acting really weird."

I point to the amulet beneath my sweater. "This thing has powers. Powers I can't control."

Ivy's eyes light up. "What kind of powers?"

"I don't know. Powers. Like I think something, and it just happens."

"Like what?"

I tell her about Miss A's hair, about her hair, about Jo's bacon, and my conversation with Kendall last night.

"I told her she'd need me, and bam! Today she's my research partner. And, trust me, this girl needs me to get this report done. I don't think she's ever completed a single assignment without her friends' help. She's never once made the honor roll. I don't mean to brag, but having me as a partner guarantees she'll get an A. Even if she doesn't earn it."

I can practically hear the gears in Ivy's head spinning faster and faster. "Wait a minute. *You're* the reason I left my hair down?"

I shrug. "I don't know. I think so."

"Don't ever do that again!" Ivy points a finger at me. "Do you know how much I've been teased today?"

"Whatever. Your hair looks wonderful."

Ivy pulls her curly hair down in an attempt to control it. "Have you *looked* at me?"

I force my eyes to focus on Ivy's hair. This morning her hair was still damp, and the curls around her face were soft and loose. Now her hair is a puffy, frizzy mess.

"I'm sorry," I tell her. "Honest."

"This is why I never wear my hair down. I forgot how much I hated it."

"It won't happen again. Promise."

She gives me a grin that lets me know she isn't mad.

"Let's go find your custodian," she says, linking her arm in mine. "I'm going to have to keep a close eye on you, aren't I?"

We walk the halls, doing our best to ignore the empty rumbling in our stomachs.

We pass several custodians—one in the GC, one in the lobby, and one in the bathroom.

"Are you sure you remember what she looks like?" Ivy asks.

"Positive."

We turn the corner to the wing of the building containing our classrooms and run into a cleaning cart. I don't see a custodian, so I look in the classrooms around us, but all of them are empty.

"Dang it," I whisper to Ivy. "Where is she?"

A heavily accented voice speaks behind us, nearly giving both of us heart attacks. "Can I help you find something?"

We turn around, and I practically jump up and down. It's her.

"No, thank you," Ivy says.

Ivy begins to walk away, but I stay where I am, memorizing her face and her nametag. Esme.

"Are you sure you're okay?" she asks me. "You look like you've seen a ghost."

Ivy turns around to see where I am and realizes I've found my custodian.

"I'm fine, thank you."

Get her keys.

"Um—"

She pulls a spray bottle with blue liquid from the cart, but looks at me before moving on to the classroom she's cleaning.

I look at the keys dangling from her wrist on a coiled cord. I need those keys. My fingers itch to snatch them and run.

"Do you think . . . ," I begin, not at all sure what I'm about to ask her. What was our plan again? "I left something in Lady Jennica's classroom. Can I borrow your keys to get in?"

The custodian smiles and rolls the keys off her arm. "I'll let you in."

My heart hits the floor. I give Ivy a *Do something* look.

"Which classroom?" Esme asks, large key between her fingers.

The bell rings, signaling the end of lunch, and the hallway begins filling with students.

"You should be able to get in now," she says, pulling the key cord back up her arm.

Ivy grabs my hand. "Let's go."

She drags me around the corner and speaks softly as girls begin walking past us to class. "You can't just ask her for the keys."

She's right, of course. What was I thinking? We're going to have to borrow them. Without permission. And that's not stealing, because we're totally going to return them.

"We have to come up with a good plan to get them." I put my hand over the amulet, buried beneath two layers of clothing. "Because this thing is freaking me out."

In elements class Lady Rose calls girls to her desk, where they talk in private about what they've written in their journal. I look at my own journal in disappointment. I'm feeling and experiencing so much more than I've written down. But I can't make myself put it on paper. I thought I was coming to Dowling to learn how to be a hedge witch, learn skills that would require me to use plants to help people. Sure, I thought it was a little boring as far as witches go, but after these past couple of days, boring sounds perfect.

Lady Rose walks with Jo to the lab area of our classroom. Every pair of eyes in the room follows. This is the first girl she's taken to the lab. Does it mean she knows what Jo's power is?

Lady Rose opens the storage room door, and Jo walks inside. The teacher shuts the door behind her.

"Hallie, Ivy," she calls to us. "Can you please go into the restroom at the end of the hall? Have a short conversation about any topic you choose. Then come back."

I glance at Ivy, unsure what to do.

Ivy is already standing. "Let's go," she whispers.

I follow her out of the classroom, and we speed-walk to the bathroom.

Once inside, we just look at each other, then burst out laughing.

"Awkward," she says.

"What are we supposed to talk about?"

She shrugs. "Anything. Let's talk about . . ."

"Movies," I answer.

"Okay. What's your favorite movie?"

"*The Incredibles.* Yours?"

"*Hoot.*"

"Think that's enough?" I ask.

"She said short," Ivy says. She swings the door open, and we walk back to the classroom.

Lady Rose is in the same place, standing in front of the storage room door.

"Did you do as I asked?"

We both nod. "Yes, ma'am."

"Very well," she says, opening the storage room door.

Jo walks out smiling.

Lady Rose looks at Jo. "Did the test work?"

Jo nods, then looks at me, half-laughing. "Are you serious? Your favorite movie is *The Incredibles*? What are you, eight?"

My mouth drops open. How did she hear that?

Lady Rose looks to me. "What did you ladies talk about?"

"Movies," I answer. "Our favorite movies."

"And yours is *The Incredibles*?"

I nod numbly. How could Jo have possibly heard us?

Lady Rose turns to Jo again. "What was Ivy's favorite movie?"

Every pair of eyes in the room is locked on Jo. I know what she's going to say before she says it.

"*Hoot.*"

Ivy slaps her hand to her chest. "That's right! How'd you know that?"

Jo is beaming like a fluorescent light. This is what she's been waiting for. *Real* magic.

"Seekers," Lady Rose says, putting one hand on Jo's shoulder. "Jo has been blessed with the gift of clairaudience."

Clairaudience?

I look at Ivy, but she looks as clueless as me.

"What does that mean?" asks Dru, her black eyes wide and her face animated in curiosity.

"It means Jo can hear what people say even when they are far away."

"Wow," Dru says. "Cool."

Lady Rose laughs lightly. "You're right; it is cool. Let's not forget, however, that our goal as Seekers is to not only find our gift, our *karama*, but also to develop it. Learning your gift can be overwhelming. Jo will have to learn how to control what she can hear."

My mind scrambles back to the conversations I've had with Ivy. What has Jo heard? Does she know I have the amulet?

"I don't really like the idea that someone can hear what I'm saying. What if it's secret?" a girl asks.

"Sweet girl, you're in a school for witches. There's nothing you can do or say or think that won't be detected by someone in this building."

A hot flush runs through my body. Then my hands begin to sweat.

Ivy snaps her fingers at me. "Chill," she mouths.

I shake my head at her. Nothing about this is okay.

Jo sits back down in her seat, and Lady Rose calls another girl to her desk. I'm shocked by how calmly Lady Rose handles Jo's gift. I wonder if I'll ever get so used to people having special powers that it doesn't totally freak me out.

I look at Jo, who's talking to Dru. She doesn't act like she knows about the amulet. Maybe she didn't have the gift then. *Please, please, please* let that be true.

"Hallie," Lady Rose calls, motioning me to her desk.

I put my journal down in front of her.

She opens it, then frowns. "Should I know what these things mean?"

I give her a nervous smile. "I wasn't sure what to write."

It's kind of a lie, but I'm too scared to tell her the truth.

I look back at Jo. If she could hear me in the bathroom, she can definitely hear in the same room.

"Don't worry about Jo," she says softly. "I've blocked her from hearing our conversation."

My eyes widen.

"Yes, I can do that," she adds.

I let out a deep breath and feel my body relax.

"So tell me what these things mean," she says, pointing to my journal.

"It's kind of weird, and it might just be a coincidence, so I'm not even sure it's really happening."

"Why don't you share them with me, and we'll figure it out together."

She listens patiently as I tell her about the headmistress repeating my thoughts, about Miss A dying her hair, and Ivy leaving her hair down and about Jo throwing away the bacon. I tell her how all these things happened after I thought about them happening. I tell her about everything.

Except the amulet.

When I finish, she looks at me intently, like she's trying

to figure me out. My stomach clenches. Am I going to be the one girl at Dowling no one can figure out?

We sit in awkward silence for a minute or two.

She finally shakes her head, like she's waking from a dream. "I'm sorry, Hallie. I was just thinking."

"Do you know what this means?" I ask quietly, still unconvinced Jo can't hear me.

Lady Rose nods slowly. "If this means what I think it does," she says, putting her hand on mine, "You're much more special than anyone predicted."

Fourteen

What'd she say?" Ivy whispers to me at the end of the school day.

My eyes search for Jo. I don't want her to hear this. But she can hear anything from anywhere.

I enter the library, and Ivy follows me.

"I'm supposed to meet Kendall here to work on the research project," I say.

Ivy drops her bag on a table. "Don't even think about avoiding my question. What did Lady Rose say to you?"

I plop into a hard wooden chair and bang my head on the table. "I don't want to tell you."

Ivy sits across from me. "Come on. It can't be that bad. Tell me what she said."

I look up at my friend, whose hair has expanded at

least six inches since the last time I looked at it. I shouldn't have wished that Ivy would leave her hair down. I should have listened to her. Now she's getting teased, and it's entirely my fault.

"She gave me an assignment," I say finally. "To test my gift."

Ivy bounces in her seat. "That's awesome! What's your gift? You're a hedge witch, right?"

I shake my head. "Lady Rose thinks I have the gift of mind manipulation."

Ivy looks at me, face blank. "What does that even mean?"

"It means I can control what people think."

"Get out!" Ivy says, slapping her hands on the table. "That's so cool!"

"Not so much," I say.

"I'd *love* to control what people think. I could make people like me, or treat me a certain way, or even give me something I wanted. That's way better than Jo's gift."

I think about what she says. Maybe she's right. Maybe mind manipulation isn't as bad as I thought.

"If this is your gift, you'll have all kinds of power."

Do I really want this much power? Dad always said

power comes with responsibility. What if I can't handle it?

"What's your assignment?"

I open my bag and pull out my journal. I read Lady Rose's perfect handwriting under my notes.

"Focus on something to happen.

Say it out loud three times."

"That's it? That's all you have to do?"

"According to Lady Rose."

"Wait," Ivy says. "I thought you were supposed to be some sort of garden witch."

I smile at my friend, grateful I have her. "Hedge witch."

"Yeah, that. What happened with that?"

"Lady Rose said everyone assumed I'd inherited my great-great-grandmother's gift, but this happens some-times."

"So . . . ," Ivy says, smile on her face.

"So?" I ask in return.

"So what are you going to wish for?"

"I don't know. I haven't really thought about it."

"You have to do something to Kendall. Or Zena! Please do something to one of them. They totally deserve it!"

I shake my head. "I'm not going to wish for anything bad to happen. Not even to Kendall and Zena."

Ivy sits back in her chair, disappointed.

"Remember the rule? No dark magic. I have to ask for something good to happen."

With a frustrated sigh she says, "What a waste."

"Any clue about your gift?" I ask.

"Nope. I've got nothing. Maybe I'm a defective witch."

"Doubtful."

She shrugs, like she doesn't really care what her gift is. But I know better. I know she's worried because she hasn't discovered her gift. "I wonder what Kendall's and Zena's powers are," she says.

"I pray neither one of them have mind manipulation." A shiver runs through me. "Can you imagine them with that power?"

I look at the clock behind Ivy's head. Kendall is ten minutes late.

"Think she's going to show?" Ivy asks.

"Doubt it. But I'm going to wait ten more minutes just to make sure."

"Well, I'm not waiting with you. See you at dinner."

I watch Ivy walk out of the library. Then I touch the amulet, ready to complete my assignment. I'm surprisingly relaxed.

I focus on only one thing, on the one girl I want to help. Ivy.

"Let Ivy's power be known.

"Let Ivy's power be known.

"Let Ivy's power be known."

When I enter the dining room, I look for Ivy, hoping my thoughts, or spell, or whatever I did, worked. I walk to where she sits and find an empty seat. She's almost never late.

Zena looks up at me, irritation in her dark eyes. "When I left her in our room, she was crying her eyes out. It wasn't pretty."

My heart freezes in my chest.

"Crying? Why is she crying? What did you do to her?"

"Ease up, dork. I didn't do anything."

The headmistress is standing on the stage, prepared to begin blessing the food. I notice Miss A looking at me with concern. I point to Ivy's empty chair, and she nods in understanding. I walk to my seat and sit between Kendall and Dru.

The headmistress begins the blessing, but my mind can't focus on anything she's saying. I'm too worried about Ivy.

When dinner is delivered to the table, I push the food around on my plate, my once hungry stomach now knotted in fear. What if my wish caused this? What if it went all wrong? It's not like I know what I'm doing.

I race out of the dining room as soon as the plates are picked up, and go to Ivy's room. I knock and call her name simultaneously.

"Ivy!" *Knock, knock, knock.*

"It's me. Hallie." *Knock, knock, knock.*

When the door opens a crack, I walk through it and follow Ivy back to her unmade bed.

I sit on the bed next to her. Her eyes are puffy from crying, and she looks miserable. Like someone-ran-over-my-dog miserable.

"What happened?" I ask her, fury heating my face. "What did Zena do?"

She shakes her head. "I don't know. When I left the library, I came back to my room to study. Zena was here reading but didn't say anything to me. Everything was normal. Then all of a sudden I felt so scared and so alone. I've never felt that way. Never."

"And you began crying."

Ivy nods.

"When did you stop?" I ask her.

"About the time dinner started. I feel better now, but my eyes are a mess. They'll be swollen in the morning, too."

The door opens and Miss A walks in, plate of food in one hand, a glass of tea in the other. I look at the door, watch it close by itself behind her. One day I'm going to learn how to do that.

"Thank you," Ivy says.

Miss A places the food and drink on Ivy's desk and sits in the chair. "Are you feeling okay?" She places a chubby hand on Ivy's forehead. "No fever."

"I'm better now," Ivy says.

"Well, you didn't miss a doggone thing at dinner. Did she, Hallie?"

I shake my head, barely able to remember dinner because I was so worried about Ivy.

"You know, getting used to life at Dowling can be hard," Miss A says. "And you've got it tougher than most, rooming with this one." She points behind her to Zena's bed.

For a second I want to argue that I've got it worse because of Kendall, but I hold my tongue. This isn't the time to engage in a war over who has the worst roommate.

148

"I know you don't have it much easier," Miss A says to me with a wink. "Trust me, girls, this will work out. It always does."

Ivy and I nod our heads in pretend agreement. I will never see the value of us having to room with Kendall and Zena.

Miss A looks at the plate of food, then smacks her forehead. "I forgot the dessert. What was I thinking?" She looks at the plate, then turns her hand the same way she did when Ivy fainted.

*"Let this plate expand and make
room for a triple-layer cake."*

In an instant a slice of triple-layer chocolate cake is sitting on the plate.

Ivy's mouth falls open. "How did you—?"

"Easy as pie. Or should I say 'cake'?" She giggles at herself. "You'll be able to do that in no time."

When Miss A leans forward to give Ivy a hug, I see a patch of hairless skin on the back of her head. I gasp at the sight of it.

"Miss A!"

"What's wrong, sugar?" Miss A asks, pulling away from Ivy.

"There's a spot—"

"A spot? Where?" she asks, looking at her blouse. "I always get food on myself. My sister always said I was messier than a hog in slop."

"Not there," I say, then point to her head. "There."

She puts a hand to the back of her head. When she feels the two-inch-wide circle of soft scalp beneath her fingers, she yelps like a dog whose tail has been stepped on.

She races to the bathroom, then yelps again.

Miss A comes out of the bathroom, her normally cheerful face twisted in horror. "She said this might happen, but I never dreamed . . ."

"Who said what?" I asked.

"Rhonda, my hairdresser. She's a dorm mom on the third floor and loves to do hair. She said I might have some minor hair loss."

Ivy shakes her head. "That's a little more than 'minor' hair loss, Miss A."

"If you girls are all right, I'm going to see her now. I can't very well have this spot showing. Even an old lady like me can be vain."

"We're fine," says Ivy. "Thank you for bringing dinner."

"And for the cake," I add, smiling.

"Anything for my girls," Miss A says, walking quickly to the door. As she's walking out of the room, I hear her mutter, "I knew I shouldn't have dyed my hair. I don't know what possessed me to do it."

Fifteen

Ivy sits with Lady Rose at the front of the room. All day Ivy has been a total wreck. Crying one minute, elated the next. Even now, as she's talking to Lady Rose, her eyes are watery, and Lady Rose rubs her back in comfort.

I've been waiting for Ivy's gift to appear, but nothing magical has happened yet. All day I've been disappointed but relieved. Mind manipulation is not what I want for my gift. But if it is my gift, I might be able to make things better for Ivy.

Lady Rose stands and pulls Ivy up with her, holding Ivy around the shoulders as if she might run away. Ivy looks calmer than she has all day and gives me a small smile.

"Seekers, I need your attention."

The room falls silent, and everyone looks at Lady Rose and Ivy.

"We have discovered Ivy's gift."

I look at Ivy, and she nods her head in agreement. Ivy knows her gift?

Wait. That means my wish came true.

No, no, no, no, no.

"Ivy has the very special gift of empathy. It means she can feel what other people around her are feeling."

Ivy's skin is still blotchy from being mad at lunch for an unknown reason, and it all makes sense. The crying last night . . . after I made the wish that her gift be revealed. But whose feelings were making her cry last night? Zena's? She doesn't even seem capable of that emotion.

Lady Rose squeezes Ivy closer to her. "As Ivy learns how to control the emotions she is bombarded by, we all need to be patient and understanding. The gift of empathy can be extremely upsetting at times."

Ivy rolls her eyes at me, and I have to giggle just a little. "Ya think?" she mouths to me.

I'm relieved to see her sense of humor shine through. She walks back to her desk and sits down, all eyes on her.

"Okay, girls," Lady Rose says. "Back to work."

The class settles back into something like normalcy, and I turn in my seat to face to Ivy. "You okay?"

Ivy nods. "Just glad I'm not going crazy. I really thought that was what was happening."

I put my hand on hers and squeeze. "We'll figure it out, okay?"

She smiles at me. "Thanks."

"Hallie Simon," Lady Rose calls.

"My turn," I whisper.

I grab my journal and walk to the front of the room. Each step I take makes me a little more anxious. I don't want Lady Rose to confirm what I already know.

"So tell me, Hallie, what did you think about last night? What did you wish for?"

I open my journal and point to the three lines I wrote after I said them out loud.

Let Ivy's power be known.
Let Ivy's power be known.
Let Ivy's power be known.

Reading the words to myself, I know—and hate—what it means.

Lady Rose sits back in her chair and scrutinizes me like she's never seen me before. "When did you say these words? Before or after Ivy began crying last night?"

"Before," I whisper.

Lady Rose shakes her head, a stunned smile on her face. "Well, what do you know?"

I look at my teacher, trying to figure out what she means, but her face is unreadable.

"You, Seeker Hallie, have a most unique gift. Mind manipulation is rare. So rare that I've only known one other witch to have it. It's a tricky gift, you know."

I know, all right. Look what I did to Ivy's and Miss A's hair. And I didn't exactly do Ivy any favors bringing her gift to life. She's an emotional mess now.

"Does this mean I won't be a hedge witch?" I ask.

Lady Rose smiles sympathetically, her face soft and kind. "No, Hallie. I'm sorry. You won't be a hedge witch. You'll be much more powerful than a hedge witch."

"I don't like this gift," I tell her. "I wish for something good to happen, and it turns out all wrong."

She pats my hand. "It's okay. It'll get easier. I'll help you."

I wish I could turn back time and go home. I would refuse to come to Dowling. No one should have this kind of power. Especially not me. I'm only eleven!

Lady Rose stands and motions for me to stand next to her. I don't want her to announce my gift. *Please don't announce my gift*, I think, eyes closed. *Please.*

Lady Rose looks at me and winks. "Nice try."

I stare at her in shock. Did she hear what I just said?

"Seekers, Hallie has discovered her gift."

Everyone in the room waits anxiously to hear what it is. Even Kendall and Zena are watching through hateful, but undeniably curious, eyes.

"Hallie's gift is rare. Very rare. And very powerful. It's a gift she will spend months learning how to control." She stops, looks at me with a smile. "Hallie's gift is mind manipulation."

Zena's face turns red, like a giant tomato. It brings me some mean sense of satisfaction that she is so upset. Kendall's face is blank, unreadable.

"Mind manipulation is the ability to influence what others think and do," Lady Rose says.

Every girl in the room looks at me suspiciously. Like they're attempting to block me from their brains. Like I'm a freak.

"Everyone can relax," Lady Rose says. "I'll be working very closely with Hallie to help her manage her gift. And we all know Hallie. She's kind and compassionate. She wouldn't wish harm on any of you."

Lady Rose pushes my back gently and hands me my journal. "Careful with your thoughts, okay?"

I nod, then walk back to my desk, every eye in the room watching every step I make.

I sit down next to Ivy and sigh loudly.

She looks at me with serious eyes, and I know she's experiencing my gut-twisting fear. "It's okay," she says. "We're in this together."

As the weeks pass, dinner becomes more and more entertaining. As Seekers learn their gifts, weird things happen.

One night a girl was pointing at a small dish of butter, asking another girl to pass it to her. Before the girl could touch the dish, it slid all the way down the table to the girl pointing to it. It snapped to her finger like it was the world's strongest magnet. That brought a round of applause, and she spent the rest of the evening zapping things to her.

Tonight, just as our dishes are being brought out, the girl on the other side of Kendall begins floating out of her chair. Her roommate pulls her back down and holds her in place until Miss A can get a seat belt. Turns out the power of levitation is hard to control.

When Miss A scoots past us to buckle the girl in, she whispers something into the girl's ear to make her smile. Miss A is always helping others. She may be a little eccentric, but I've never met anyone sweeter.

Kendall barely notices the girl levitating next to her. Like on every other night, she ignores the activity around her and pushes the food around on her plate, eating only a bite or two of each meal.

Tonight, however, she's more serious than ever.

I lean a few inches closer to her. "Wild, huh?"

Kendall's fork stops moving, but she doesn't look at me.

The familiar stab of rejection pierces my chest.

Why do I keep doing this to myself? Kendall will never change.

"Remember," I tell her, "we have to work on our research project tonight. We only have a week left."

She has managed to put me off or stand me up since we got the assignment, and now that we are a week away from the due date, I'm starting to panic that it won't get done.

Kendall doesn't look up when she answers, "I'm busy tonight."

"You're busy every night," I shoot back. "We have to get this done. And we have to do it together."

"Not tonight," she says, shooting me a death glare.

The slow burn of frustration heats my face.

"If you don't help with the project, I'll make sure Lady Jennica knows."

Kendall doesn't acknowledge me, doesn't look at me, doesn't even blink.

I turn to Dru, who is watching the little bursts of magic happening around her. "Jeez, I wish I knew what my gift was," she says.

"Don't be so anxious," I tell her. "You may not like it."

Dru's big black eyes roll in exaggeration. "Whatever. Like you don't like your gift. You can make things happen. You can change people. Anyone would kill for that gift."

I look at Dru. "Right. Sure they would."

"Ask anyone," she says.

The girls around her nod in agreement. Even Jo.

What if Dru's right, and I'm looking at this all wrong?

Maybe my gift is exactly what I need.

Maybe my gift can change Kendall.

Sixteen

I look at the note in my hand one last time before leaving my room. Ivy had handed it to me after dinner, then raced off to her room before I could talk to her.

Meet me in the Seeker Sanctum at 7.

Great. The basement—again. And this time I'm going alone.

The hallway is quiet, most girls studying in their rooms or in the lobby. I take the narrow old steps two at a time, slowing down as I get closer to the entrance of the Seeker Sanctum. I thought I was only meeting Ivy, but the sound of barely audible voices greets me. I stop, listen carefully, thinking it must be Dru and Jo, but when I sneak closer to the room's entrance, I see the two faces I spend most days trying to avoid.

Kendall and Zena are sitting cross-legged on the empty triangular stage, a large book in front of them. The seats we previously sat in are empty. One large candle sits beside them and serves as the only light in the room.

I look down the hallway behind me, but Ivy is nowhere to be seen. I fight the urge to run, to find Miss A. She'd know what to do.

But I can't leave. I have to see what they're doing.

Back against the wall, I peer around the corner in my best CSI cop stance.

Zena turns pages in the book gingerly. She's talking as she does, but it's so soft, I can't hear a thing. Where's Jo when I need her?

I look at my watch. 6:57.

Come on, Ivy.

Even with my glasses on, I can't tell what book they're looking at it. It isn't a Book of Shadows. Those are smaller, the size of a large novel. This book is the size of the extra large dictionary you can find in libraries.

Suddenly a dark feeling washes over me and I know Kendall and Zena are breaking the no-dark-magic rule.

I put my hand on the amulet hidden beneath my shirt for comfort, for guidance.

Again I'm calmed by the power it brings me. I've looked less and less for the custodian, afraid to give up the amulet. I know its power isn't truly mine, and I really shouldn't have it, but I'm scared to walk the Dowling halls without it.

A hand touches my shoulder, and another hand slaps over my mouth to stifle my scream. I turn to see Ivy and, close behind her, Jo and Dru.

Ivy pushes me behind her and takes a look at the pair in a closet next to the Seeker Sanctum. Then she motions for us to move down the hall, closer to the main hallway.

Her voice a whisper, Ivy says, "I had a feeling something was going to happen today. Then Jo told me she overheard Kendall and Zena saying they were meeting at seven. Did you see anything?"

I shake my head and wonder how I missed these conversations. Where was I when she and Jo were talking about this? They hang out without me? I feel a tiny stab of jealousy but push it aside.

Sweet little Dru looks as confused as I do. "When did you hear that?" she asks her roommate. "And why didn't you tell me?"

"If I told you everything I heard," Jo says, "you'd get sick of hearing me talk. I'm already sick of listening to everyone else."

Ivy leads us back down the hallway silently.

We attempt to position ourselves to see inside the room, but only the first person in our group can really see in without being caught. Jo hangs back, able to hear what she wants without seeing Kendall and Zena.

I try to think of something I can wish for, something I can make Kendall and Zena think or do that will make it easier for us to spy on them. But I draw a complete blank.

Great. I have one of the most powerful gifts in Dowling history, and it's as useless as an ashtray on a motorcycle.

Ivy watches closely, her body frozen in position. Dru stands behind me and picks at her nails. I do my best to hear Kendall and Zena, but their whispers are too soft to understand.

Jo grabs Dru and starts walking away. I tap Ivy's shoulder and point down the hall, motioning that we need to go, but she shakes me off and keeps watching.

I'm stuck, not sure if I should stick with Ivy or leave with the other girls. Common sense says I should race back to my room and act like I wasn't here, but I stay with Ivy. She's the only real friend I have, and I'm not going to abandon her.

The candle in the sanctum blows out, drowning us in

complete darkness. Ivy spins around to leave, tripping over me and nearly falling. I grab her hand to steady her. Then we fly down the narrow hallway as quietly as we can. Once we're up the stairs, Jo motions to us from her door. We race to their room and close the door behind us.

Everyone looks as freaked out as I feel. The only person halfway collected is Ivy.

Ivy sits on one of the beds, and I sit next to her. Dru and Jo sit on the other bed. Their room is identical to mine and Ivy's but smells like bubble gum. Since we aren't allowed to have candy, I'm curious who snuck it in and how it hasn't been discovered. But this isn't the time to ask about gum.

"What just happened back there?" I ask shakily.

Ivy's the first to answer. "I could tell Zena was up to something because her mood shifted dramatically. She went from being sad and desperate to excited. *Really* excited. Her adrenaline has been pumping through me all day."

Dru leans forward. "Really? Man, that's so cool!"

Ivy shakes her head. "It's exhausting."

"Then I heard Kendall and Zena talking in the bathroom today," Jo says. "They were planning to meet in the Sanctum to do some spell. Zena insisted they use the *Grimoire*."

"That sounds familiar. What is it?" I ask.

Ivy looks at me. "The *Grimoire*. Lady Silver mentioned it in history."

"What's so special about it?" Dru asks.

"It's like the master spell book," Ivy says. "It contains spells we'll learn and perform, and spells no one should ever perform. It's got every good and bad spell known to Dowling."

"What did they say? What kind of spell did they attempt?" I ask.

Ivy looks at Jo for answers. It all makes sense now. Jo was needed to hear what we couldn't.

Jo closes her eyes, repeating the words she heard.

"Take beauty from my enemies and make them now see
That no one is better or prettier than me.
Droop their eyes and misshape their hair,
Until no one will look at them, not even on a dare.
Replace their smiles with disfigured teeth
And let all their faults be visible to see."

No one breathes. No one speaks.

Jo opens her eyes slowly. "You were right," she tells Ivy. "They were up to no good."

"How did you remember all that?" Ivy asks.

Jo shrugs. "I don't know. I just did."

"So what does it mean?" I ask. "Are we going to wake up ugly and disfigured?"

My hand instinctively touches my perfect teeth. And I was worried about a pimple on my nose.

Ivy laughs, tapping her braces. "My teeth are already a mess."

"Why do they hate me?" Dru asks, eyes wide in fear. "I haven't done anything to either one of them."

Jo shakes her head. "It isn't you they're talking about."

"It's us," Ivy says, gesturing to herself and me.

Jo nods in agreement.

"Well, great. Just great," I say, jumping to my feet, desperate to do something to change the spell, to make sure it doesn't work.

"Relax," Ivy says. "The odds of them getting the spell right are pretty slim. They didn't have the tools they needed for the spell anyway. I think they were just practicing."

"Hate to break it to you, " Jo says, "but they were doing it for real. I don't know how important it is to have the tools you're talking about, but if either one of them has been blessed as a master spell crafter, I'm not sure the tools matter."

My breaths are short and shallow, and I see Ivy's face

getting flushed, obviously feeling what I'm feeling.

"Calm down," she orders. "You're going to make me hyperventilate."

I take some deep breaths to slow my heartbeat, and we both relax.

"So now what do we do?" Dru asks.

"You two aren't going to do anything," I tell them. "You don't need to get involved with those two."

Jo grins. "I think it's a little late for that, seeing as how I just invaded their spell."

Nervous giggles consume us.

"Hallie's right," Ivy says. "We don't do anything. We act like nothing happened, and when we wake up in the morning and nothing has changed, we laugh."

"And if something *has* changed?" Dru asks.

"It won't," I say. *It can't.*

I look at the clock on the desk. "I need to work on my ancestry research," I say. Even though I'm not going to be a hedge witch, anything's better than thinking about what's going to happen to me.

Ivy walks with me to the door.

Before we leave, I look back at Dru and Jo. "Thanks for being such good friends."

"And remember," Ivy adds, "not a peep to anyone."

Dru gives us a sharp salute.

Ivy closes the door behind us and walks with me to my room.

"Well?" she asks. "Nervous?"

I roll my eyes at her. "*Psh.* I have curses put on me all the time."

"Yeah," she says, smiling. "Stupid question."

When we get to my room, she follows me inside. Kendall isn't back yet, and the scared little girl in me wonders what she's doing.

"I've been thinking," Ivy says.

"About?"

"The amulet."

My hand covers the amulet protectively. I'm not giving it up. Not yet.

"I think maybe you should keep it. At least for a little while."

"Really?" I ask. "I've been thinking the same thing. Especially now, with Kendall and Zena casting spells on us."

Ivy looks at me seriously. "If something changes, we go to Miss A. We tell her everything. We tell her about the amulet, and we tell her about what we saw tonight. Deal?"

I think carefully. If anyone can keep me from getting expelled for taking the amulet, it's Miss A.

I nod at my first real best friend. "Deal."

Seventeen

I'm awake long before my alarm goes off. I'm terrified to see what I look like today. Sure, Kendall and Zena are about as clueless as me when it comes to spells, but what if it worked? What if I'm covered in warts or my hair is gray or my nose has grown long and pointed?

I lift my hands to feel my face, then stop. I don't want to feel the horrifying bumps and crooked teeth.

When the alarm finally sounds, I turn it off. Kendall doesn't budge. I look at her in bed, at her flawless complexion, perfect hair, and model-worthy face. I don't know why she has hated me all these years or why she'd want me to be disfigured. It isn't like I'm a threat to her popularity.

Never have been, never will be.

I throw the sheets back, grab my glasses, and force my

feet to walk to the bathroom. I go inside but don't turn the light on. I stand there, in the dark, preparing myself for what I'm going to see.

Hand on the light switch, I close my eyes.

I flip the switch on, but can't make myself look.

I'm not ready to face my new face.

Just do it!

One eyelid cracks open, and I can see dark hair. My hair. I breathe a sigh of relief and let my eyes open slowly. When I lock eyes with the image in the mirror, relief is replaced with shock.

I lean in closer to the mirror, touch my face. My milky-smooth face. The pimple on my nose is gone. And the chicken pox scar on my forehead is a memory.

Gone are the never-been-plucked brows I'm used to seeing. In their place are the perfectly arched eyebrows of a movie star. Surrounding my eyes are the longest, darkest eyelashes I've ever seen.

And my hair . . . *my hair!*

What used to be boring brown hair with weird waves and frayed split ends is now soft, silky hair with light brown highlights. It sits perfectly on my shoulders, like someone's been working on my hair for hours.

Even my teeth are straighter than a witch's wand, and so white, they'd stop traffic.

Ivy! I have to see her. I have to see if she's been changed like me overnight.

I leave the bathroom, get my clothes from the dresser, and return to the bathroom. I half-expect to see the old me, thinking my eyes played tricks on me. But the new Hallie, the stop-you-in-your-tracks stunning Hallie, is still there.

I get dressed quickly, then brush my teeth. I don't bother touching my hair, because it's perfect. Anything I do to it will only make it worse.

Kendall is still asleep, and I tiptoe out of the room as quietly as possible and race to Ivy's door. The hallway is practically empty, and I keep my face down. I don't want to draw attention until I see Ivy. I lightly rap on her door. Seconds later the door cracks open. Ivy squints through the space, then swings it wide open when she sees me.

"Omigod!" she whispers. "Look at us!"

Ivy has changed even more dramatically. Her hair is down, but instead of puffy, out-of-control frizzy curls, her long red hair is in perfect ringlets around her face. I reach out to touch her hair, and it's so soft, it's like putting my hand through silk threads. No tangles and no frizz.

She smiles wide, and the metal braces are gone, replaced by the most perfect teeth I've ever seen.

Ivy grabs the bag behind her and joins me in the hallway. She puts a finger to her mouth to quiet me as we walk to the dining room. It's so early, we're the only girls in here except the cooks.

We grab a seat and look at each other like we've never met.

Ivy's freckles only make her impeccable face more adorable. Like me, her eyelashes and eyebrows are pure perfection. Together we look like models for *Seventeen* magazine.

"H-how—" Ivy stutters.

I shrug, confused. "It doesn't make sense. Their spell was supposed to make us ugly. I thought I'd wake up with warts the size of gumballs on my face."

Ivy giggles. "I told you they didn't know what they were doing."

"Oh. My. Gosh. Can you imagine what Kendall and Zena are going to do when they see us?"

Ivy claps happily. "This is going to be so good!"

"Wait. How do we explain it?" I ask, panicking.

"Who cares?" she says, giddy.

She's right, of course. Looking like we do now, the only thing that matters is what it does to our popularity. Combine that with our newfound gifts—and Saffra's amulet—and we're going to be unstoppable.

For the first time in my life, I'm actually looking forward to seeing Kendall.

"Well, hello, ladies!" Lady Jennica says, surprised as Ivy and I enter the room. The students in the room match her wide eyes and shocked expression.

Dru runs up to Ivy and plays with her silky red curls. "Woooowww"

Jo analyzes us from her seat. A knowing look is on her face, and she seems less surprised than the others in the room. She must have heard Ivy and me talking in the dining room this morning.

"Have a seat," Lady Jennica says. I expect her to pull us aside and grill us about what happened, but she doesn't. She shooes us to our seats like everything's normal. The surprised look on her face has been replaced with her typical serene smile.

We wait a few more silent minutes as other girls enter

the room, each one looking at us suspiciously. I fidget uncomfortably under their scrutiny, but nothing compares to the moment when Kendall and Zena walk in. Before they see us, the looks on their faces are smug, superior, secretive.

Then they see us.

The color drains from Kendall's well-tanned face. Then her skin turns a maddened red.

Even Zena, who never skips a beat, stops dead and stares at us.

What I wouldn't give to read their minds right now.

I don't look away uncomfortably as I normally would. I want Kendall to see just how wrong her spell went.

"Okay," Lady Jennica says. "Have a seat, ladies. It's time to begin."

Kendall and Zena move like zombies to their seats, like they're in a dream. A really bad dream where their enemies are suddenly prettier than they are.

"It's research time, ladies," Lady Jennica says. Half the class groans, but I don't. I haven't done a bit of research on Dannabelle, and I'm anxious to dive in. Even if Kendall doesn't do her part.

"Move seats so that you're sitting next to your research partner," she instructs.

I don't move, expecting Kendall to move closer to me. Of course, she sits frozen in place until Lady Jennica forces her to move. Kendall grabs her backpack angrily and stomps over to Ivy's desk.

I turn my desk so that we're facing one another.

"Have you done any research?" I ask, as sweet as pie.

Kendall looks up at me. "What do you think?"

I refuse to let her see me mad, so I slap another fake smile onto my now perfect face. "No worries. I haven't either, but I did get these books from the library."

I pull three books from my bag and place them between us.

Kendall pulls one of the books closer to her and fans the pages mindlessly.

"I guess we should start with history," I say, smile plastered on my face.

"Joy," she mumbles.

I reach across the table, open the book to Dannabelle's history for Kendall, and point. "There you go." I drop some notecards on the desk. "Make your notes here."

"I know what to do, loser," Kendall growls.

I ignore her like she has ignored me so many times. Opening another book, I begin reading and writing notes on notecards. I pay little attention to Kendall, but I can feel her glare drilling holes into my head. She can't keep her eyes off me. It takes everything I have not to laugh. I've finally beat Kendall at her own game. And the best part is, I didn't have to do a thing. She did it to herself.

When my pencil breaks, I look in my bag for a new one. I can't help but notice with total glee that my hair is falling in front of my face in beautiful satin sheets. When I look up, I do what I've seen Kendall do a gazillion times. I toss my hair back and let it fall into place.

I can practically hear the *I hate you* thoughts running through Kendall's head.

I never dreamed I'd be living this moment . . . where I'm just as pretty as Kendall, more powerful than Kendall, and—for once in my life—don't need Kendall in order to be popular.

Eighteen

At the beginning of elements class, Lady Rose asks to speak with me outside the room. My hands immediately begin sweating, which is so gross. But being called into the hallway is never a good thing.

Classroom door shut, Lady Rose speaks softly. "Can you hold this for me?" she asks.

I look down at the small broach in her hand. I noticed her wearing it previously, and seeing it up close now, I realize it's an elaborate broach with different-colored stones set inside it. "Sure," I say, unsure why I would need to hold it but too scared to ask.

Lady Rose looks at me closely. "Everything okay, Hallie?"

I look at her carefully. Is she trying to get something

out of me? Does she know what Kendall and Zena did last night?

I nod and smile. "Everything's fine, Lady Rose."

She puts her hand on my hair. "I couldn't help but notice the change in you and Ivy today. Did you happen to use your gift to help you with this?"

The weight of the amulet pulls on my neck. "No, ma'am. I'm not even sure how I would do that. Doesn't mind manipulation just change what people think?"

Lady Rose narrows her eyes like she's trying to figure something out. "Normally. I just wonder how this happened. Don't get me wrong. I think you look beautiful, you both do. But Dowling frowns upon Seekers dabbling in spells they haven't yet been taught."

I look at Lady Rose and struggle with what to say next. Do I rat out Kendall and Zena, or do I keep playing dumb? Ratting them out would make me so happy, but what if Lady Rose reverses the spell and we go back to *normal*?

"I don't know how it happened. I woke up like this. So did Ivy."

"Okay," she says, arms crossed over her chest. "If you think of anything I should know, I hope you'll come talk to me."

I nod the most believable way I can. "Absolutely."

She holds out her hand, and I give her back the broach, which she fastens onto her jacket. "Thank you, Hallie."

Lady Rose opens the door, and I follow her into the room. Kendall and Zena don't even look at me as I walk past them to my seat. Ivy looks at me with a *Tell me now* look.

"It's okay," I mouth.

She doesn't look like she believes me, but I face Lady Rose. Ivy will have to wait. I can't chance Jo hearing what I tell her.

"We're taking a break from exploring our gifts and doing something a little different today," Lady Rose says.

A couple of girls sigh unhappily. Kendall and Zena are the most verbal, of course. They haven't learned what their gifts are yet, and even I'm anxious to see what happens when they do.

"Relax," Lady Rose says, holding her hands in front of her. "I promise you'll enjoy this. Today, I'm going to teach you your first spell."

A couple of girls clap, and Ivy and I give each other excited smiles.

"It's a simple spell but one I think you'll enjoy and use often."

"Are we going to learn how to read people's minds?" Dru asks excitedly, her legs swinging a full foot from the ground. Lady Rose laughs quietly. "I'm afraid that's a gift, not a spell, Dru."

Dru's legs stop swinging, but the happy expression on her face stays in place.

"Some of you may have seen doors opening and closing without being touched, or lights turning off and on with just a twirl of the hand or a snap of the fingers."

Relief washes over me. I wasn't seeing things after all.

"Today you'll learn the spell, and it's so easy, you'll have it mastered before we leave class."

Lady Rose stands in front of the room. "The secret to this spell—and all spells—is believing you can do it. If you think it's impossible, I guarantee it will never happen."

She looks at the class with a knowing smile. "First thing you need to do," she says, "is take a deep breath in."

The class inhales together.

"Now exhale."

The hiss of exhalation fills the room.

"Dru, can you join me in the front?"

Dru half-skips to the front of the room, but I can barely see her with all the people in front of me.

"Just watch as Dru demonstrates for you."

She leans down to Dru, whispers into her ear. Dru nods her head, the excitement practically popping out of her pores.

Dru's face turns uncharacteristically serious. She points a tiny finger at the door, then says, "Open the door at my command, with a twist of my hand."

She twirls her hand awkwardly, and the door swings open.

The class erupts in applause, and Dru jumps up and down. "Whoa! I did that? How do I close it?"

Lady Rose raises her hand to quiet the class. She leans in to Dru and whispers into her ear again.

Dru faces the door, pointer finger stretched out. "Close the door and do not linger, at the snap of my fingers."

She snaps her fingers, and *wham*! The door closes.

More applause and more excited jumping from Dru.

I raise my hand.

"Yes, Hallie?" Lady Rose asks.

"I've seen doors open and close without anything being said. How does that work?"

Lady Rose smiles wide. "You've been watching. I like that."

I hear Kendall's unmistakable voice in front of me. "Suck-up."

Either Lady Rose doesn't hear her or she ignores it.

"The beauty of this spell is that you don't have to say it out loud. You can say it in your head, make the hand gesture, and the door will open or close as you've commanded."

"I want to practice," a girl in the front says.

"I figured you would," says Lady Rose. "But before we do, I need to talk to you about spells.

"Spells are fun," Lady Rose begins. "But they can also be dangerous. If you don't know what you're doing, you could wreak holy havoc at Dowling by attempting spells you are not yet prepared for."

Kendall and Zena look at each other knowingly. They definitely didn't intend for us to look like runway models. Even with my glasses on, I think I'm prettier than Kendall.

"Spells will be taught to you as we feel you are ready to learn them. If you practice spells on your own, you're asking for trouble."

Lady Rose eyes me specifically, as if she is still unconvinced I didn't do something to cause our overnight makeovers.

"I can't emphasize enough how strongly you will be punished if you are found playing with spells that you haven't been taught, especially if they are dark magic spells. This first year at Dowling is all about learning your limits. You have to learn in steps, not in one big leap."

Lady Rose pauses and looks at her clueless class of Seekers.

"Any questions?"

Dru raises her hand. "Now can we practice the spell?"

"Absolutely. But before we do, know that this spell will not open a door you aren't allowed to enter. This only works on doors you're allowed to open and close. Don't ask me how it works or how the magic knows. It's just the way it is. Now grab your things and let's go to your hallway so you can practice on your own room."

The class shuffles out of the room, anxious to try their first spell. As we leave the room, Lady Rose hands us a hot-pink card with the two new spells written on them.

Kendall and I stop in front of our door but stand as far apart from one another as possible.

"I'll go first," she says.

She points at the door, says the spell out loud, then twists her hand. Before her hand is back at her side, the door is open. She again points at the door, reads the spell, and snaps her fingers, and the door closes.

Pretending to be bored, Kendall moves to the side so I can practice.

I open the door easily, then walk into the room.

From inside our room I say the spell to close the door, snap my fingers, and happily watch the door close.

Right in Kendall's face.

Nineteen

Ivy sits cross-legged on my bed. We are both in our pajamas, and the amulet is tucked neatly beneath my top.

"I'm telling you," Ivy says, "they're up to something. Jo said she heard them talking about a new spell, and I can feel it on Zena. She's planning something. Something big."

"Well, the last time she planned something big, we ended up like this," I say, framing my face with my hands.

"They were mad today, really mad. Who knows what they're trying to do tonight."

I do my best to push down the panic that rises in my chest. For years Kendall has been powerful without magical skills. What if she discovers her gift and uses it against us? But I don't say any of that out loud.

Ivy continues, "Maybe we should sneak up on them

and see what spell they're casting. Like we did last night."

"No way," I say. "We almost got busted last night. Who cares what they're doing?"

Ivy looks at me sternly. "We do."

She's right, of course. I desperately want to know what spell they're concocting tonight. But I don't want to get caught, and I don't want to get in trouble.

"Let's go to Jo's room," I say. With a flick of my wrist, the door opens, and I smile. "Still loving that."

We knock on Jo and Dru's door, but no one answers. We knock again, but still no answer. "Where would they be?" I ask Ivy.

We look down both sides of the hallway. There are some other girls in pajamas moving from room to room, but none of them are Jo or Dru. We hear shuffling feet behind us and turn to see Jo and Dru half-running toward us. The door opens, and we all tumble inside the room.

"What in the world is going on?" I ask.

Dru and Jo look at each other, then back at us.

"They're in the sanctum again."

My heart sinks when I realize what that means.

"I was right!" Ivy says, happy with herself. Then sobering seriousness takes over.

"What are they doing? Trying the same spell again?" I ask.

Dru shakes her head. "No, it's something new. It sounded like they were trying to make you unpopular."

"Me?" I ask, laughing. "Since when have I been popular?"

Jo looks at me like I'm making a joke. "You're kidding, right?"

"Uhhh, no. I'm not."

"Have you seen yourself today? Even the older girls are paying more attention to you." Jo shakes her head like she doesn't believe me. "Don't tell me you haven't noticed."

"I honestly haven't." I would love to have at least one moment in the spotlight and know about it.

"Well, people are noticing you two whether you know it or not," says Dru.

"Kendall and Zena didn't see you snooping, did they?" asks Ivy.

Dru puts her hands on her hips. "Are you kidding? No one's faster than me."

I giggle at my friend.

"What are we going to do?" Ivy asks.

"Nothing," I tell her, sounding way more sure of myself than I feel. "Absolutely nothing. They haven't been taught any extra skills. They can't cast spells without all the right tools and training."

"But Zena's mom—" Ivy argues.

"Forget the headmistress. It didn't help them yesterday, and it's not going to help them today," I say.

The room falls silent, and I take a deep breath. Everyone is looking at me for reassurance because, somehow, I've become the strong one in the group.

"Look, we'll go to bed, wake up, and everything will be the same. I'm sure of it," I say. At least I hope it will be.

Back in my room, Ivy and I are on my bed, this time reading about our ancestry. I don't know why, but it just feels safer when we're together. Dad always said there was safety in numbers.

Ivy puts her book down. "Can I see the amulet again?"

I pull the amulet from under my gown and take it off for her to see. "I haven't looked at it that much. I'm too worried someone will see me."

We both touch the stones in the necklace, looking at each intricately carved stone in amazement. "Can you imagine how long it took to make this?" I say.

"Years."

Ivy drops the amulet, and I let it rest between us. It actually feels weird not having it against my skin. "What if it works?" Ivy asks.

I look at her, confused. "What if *what* works?"

"What if their spell works and we become unpopular or something?" The worry in Ivy's voice makes me instantly angry. If I knew how, I'd curse Kendall to keep her from making other people feel like this. Maybe give her a big, fat, impossible tongue that keeps her from talking at all.

I put my hand on Ivy's. "First of all, I've got some news for you. We aren't popular."

Ivy grins at that.

"Secondly, it's not going to work. They've proven they don't know how to say a spell right. *But if it does,* who cares? We don't need Kendall and Zena in order to have friends and be happy. Kendall has made my life a nightmare since I was in third grade. I won't let her control me anymore."

The metallic click of the door unlatching stops me cold. I look down at the amulet in my hand and hold my breath, cemented in place. Pure panic pulses through me.

She's going to see the amulet.

Kendall enters the room, then stops cold when she sees us.

190

"What are *you* doing here?" she asks Ivy.

Ivy looks at me, her face as white as glue. I try to speak, but when I open my mouth, nothing comes out.

"Well?" Kendall pushes. "Why are you here? And how'd you get in?"

"Studying with Hallie," she says, looking at me blankly.

I look at the amulet in my hand, at Ivy who looks like she's seen a ghost, at Kendall who doesn't even acknowledge me. *Or the amulet.* It's like I'm not even here.

"Hello?" I say, but my voice isn't heard. No one in the room appears to see me. "Hello!" My voice is louder, more insistent. No one seems to hear me, no matter how loud I am.

"Where is she?" Kendall asks, so disgusted by me, she can't even say my name. She is practically spewing hate like an out-of-control fire hydrant.

"Ummmm," Ivy looks at me but acts like she can't see me. "She'll be back."

"Whatever," Kendall says, walking to the bathroom. Two seconds later the shower goes on, and I know I've got at least ten minutes to hide the amulet in my pillowcase before she reappears.

Ivy jumps off the bed and runs for the door like she's being chased by a herd of giant scorpions.

I drop the amulet under my gown.

"Where are you going?" I ask Ivy, and this time my voice is audible.

Ivy whips around, her hand over her heart. "What ha— Where'd you go?"

"Hello, I've been sitting here the entire time."

Ivy shakes her head maniacally. "No. No, you haven't."

"Sit down," I tell her. "You're freaking me out."

She laughs, more like a crazy person than my friend. "*I'm* freaking *you* out? That's funny!"

"I don't understand," I say. "What happened? What'd I miss?"

"One minute you're sitting across from me, the next minute you're gone."

"Gone? What do you mean gone? I didn't move."

"Well, you sure as heck weren't sitting here."

I stop talking and think. Neither one of them could hear me? I thought Kendall was just ignoring me like she always does.

"You really couldn't see me?" I ask her, voice shaking.

"How many times do I have to say it? *I* couldn't see you, and *Kendall* couldn't see you."

"You couldn't hear me either?"

She folds her arms over her chest. "No, Hallie. No. We didn't see you. We didn't hear you. Know why? Because you weren't here. You weren't here!"

Her voice is at the peak of hysteria, and I want to calm her down, but I don't have an answer for her.

I shake my head. "But I was here. I was sitting right here. I never moved."

"Then why couldn't we see you?"

I look at her, scared and confused. Her face mirrors my own feelings. Something really weird just happened. The blood in my body turns to solid ice.

"I think I became invisible."

Twenty

My mind is still spinning like a category four hurricane when I walk to history the following morning.

I'm terrified about what happened last night. Did I really turn invisible? And if I did, how did I do it? It's not like I wished to be invisible, but I *was* worried about Kendall seeing the amulet. The whole situation is too outlandish to be true, even for Dowling.

I looked up spells in my Book of Shadows to see if there is an invisibility spell, but I couldn't find one. Maybe Kendall and Zena cast that spell on me. Maybe they finally figured out how to cast spells successfully. I think about the *Grimoire* they were reading from and make a mental note to find one. Surely there's more than one copy. If I can get my hands on a copy of the *Grimoire*, I might be able to figure out what spell they put on me.

I've barely got a foot in the doorway when I hear girls in the class calling to me.

"Hi, Hallie!"

"Love your hair today, Hallie!"

"Need a study partner?"

I stop by Lady Jennica's desk, suspicious about the attention. But one look at Ivy waving me toward her furiously, and my feet are back in motion.

Every girl I pass on the way to my seat smiles, waves, or says something nice to me. The girls at Dowling have always been nice enough, but nothing like this. This is more like the attention Kendall and Zena normally receive. Everyone knows they're the popular girls. Well, maybe not popular, but powerful. They have been since day one.

I hold my hand over the amulet as I sit down. Ivy leans over and whispers into my ear. "They did the same thing to me."

I lean back and look at her. Something isn't right. Something really weird is going on. Even Lady Jennica is smiling at us instead of writing on the board or filing her nails like she normally does.

At exactly nine o'clock Kendall and Zena walk in.

They wear matching headbands, bracelets, and attitudes. Instead of being greeted with a chorus of hellos from the class, the room is silent. The unusually cold greeting gives them pause, and their smug faces fade briefly.

"Have a seat," Lady Jennica says to the pair, her tone shorter than normal. She has never really liked Kendall and Zena, but today she seems downright snippy with them.

They take their seats quickly, and Lady Jennica sits on her desk. Her dainty feet are strapped into six-inch heels that lace halfway up her leg with black satin ribbon. I can't imagine ever wearing those kinds of shoes.

But I also never thought I'd be able to make myself invisible, so what do I know?

Lady Jennica instructs us to work on our project, and while I work, I watch Kendall and Zena. They are repeatedly ignored when they make a joke, or are blown off when they ask other girls for help.

It's impossible to ignore the way the girls in class, and even Lady Jennica, are drawn to me and Ivy, like there's an invisible magnet pulling them to us. People are smiling at us for no reason, offering help we don't ask for.

Kendall keeps glaring at me, like I'm making people dis her. If I'm honest with myself, I don't hate the way people are treating me. It's nice to actually be noticed.

Kendall shifts in her seat, intermittently sighing and rolling her eyes when she can't harness the attention of anyone in the room. Even Lady Jennica has busied herself with other girls.

I sit back in my chair and absorb this feeling of being . . . important. I'm instinctively drawn again to miserable Kendall.

Now you know how it feels, I think. I turn my attention to my work and don't think of Kendall for the rest of the class period.

The closer I get to seeing Lady Rose, the more nervous I get. I have to talk to her today. I know it's not my turn, but I have to talk to her about what happened last night.

Journal in hand, I walk to her desk before class starts.

"Good afternoon, Hallie," she says softly. She sits back in her chair like she was expecting me. Maybe that's her gift. Maybe she's psychic.

"Lady Rose, would it be possible for me to speak with you today? I know it's not my turn, but this is really impor—"

She holds up her hand to stop me. "Of course. I'll call you up first."

My muscles relax in relief. "Thank you."

I walk back to my desk to a chorus of heys and hellos from every girl in the room. It's been happening all day, and it's about to drive me crazy. I used to think I wanted to be noticed, but it's exhausting smiling and talking to everyone. At this rate I'll never get a second alone to return the amulet.

I sit down next to Ivy, and she gives me a big, excited smile. "I can't believe how much attention we're getting!"

I shake my head. "*I* can't believe it's that important to you."

"Hallie Simon. You are not going to ruin my fun. We're going to enjoy every second of popularity we get. Understand?"

I laugh at this. I may not care anything about being the center of attention, but Ivy obviously does. I've enjoyed watching Kendall squirm all day, but I've never really wanted to be popular. It just seems like too much work.

Lady Rose lights the incense, and the room quickly fills with the sweet and spicy aroma that I've come to love. I used to think only hippies burned incense, but it turns out witches love the stuff too.

When Lady Rose closes the door, the class knows it's

time to get quiet. Many girls still haven't discovered their
gifts. Kendall and Zena have both spent time with Lady
Rose, but she has never announced their gifts. I wonder if
that's because they don't know their gifts or because they
asked her not to tell.

She calls my name first, and I walk quickly to her desk
with my journal.

"No one can hear us?" I ask her before I begin talking.

"No one," she assures me.

"Okay. Something weird happened last night."

She nods her head but doesn't seem surprised.

"I was talking to Ivy in my room and was showing her—"

I stop myself from telling her I was showing Ivy the
amulet.

She nods again, encouraging me to continue.

"I was showing her something, and then Kendall
walked in."

"That's your roommate, right?" she asks.

"Right," I say, then wonder how she knows that. *Witch
school*, I remind myself.

"When she walked in, I didn't want her to see me,
and I—"

I look up at Lady Rose. Can I really trust her? I have

a final battle with myself about whether or not to tell her. To tell anyone.

"What happened, Hallie?" she asks, leaning in closer, speaking in a whisper. "I know this can be scary, but you can tell me. It's okay."

I take a deep breath and, on the exhale, say in a rush, "I disappeared."

Lady Rose cocks her head to the side, like she heard me wrong. Great, now I've stumped the teacher who knows everything about witch powers and spells.

"What do you mean, you disappeared?" she asks.

"Ivy said that when Kendall walked in, I disappeared. I was invisible. She couldn't see me, my clothes, my hair. Nothing. It's like I wasn't there."

"Could you see her? Hear her?"

I nod emphatically. "That's the thing. I said something to Kendall, and they didn't hear me. I thought I was there, but I wasn't, somehow. I know this sounds crazy, and I thought my gift was mind manipulation, but maybe it's this. Maybe I'm the Incredible Invisible Girl. Maybe I'm just a freak. Maybe I—"

Lady Rose puts her hands on my shoulders. "Shh," she says softly. "Shh."

Suddenly I miss my mother so much, I want to cry.

"I thought this might happen," she says.

I sit straight up in my chair. "You did? How?"

Lady Rose looks at me, like she's not quite sure how much she should tell me.

"Am I going crazy?" I ask her. "I feel like I'm going crazy."

She chuckles and shakes her head. "No, Hallie. You are definitely not going crazy."

"Then what is it?"

My heart squeezes when she looks at me with uncertainty. I want her to know what's wrong with me. I *need* her to know.

"I'm not exactly sure yet," she tells me. She opens a drawer and pulls out a small, dainty bracelet. It's silver with little red stones in it. It looks like an antique, and I don't take it from her when she hands it to me. "Take the bracelet, Hallie."

I look at the bracelet, then at her. "What's going to happen?"

She gives me an apologetic grin. "I don't really know yet. But nothing bad will happen. I can promise you that."

She fastens the bracelet around my left wrist without

asking my permission. And I know I don't have a choice. I must wear the bracelet.

"I want you to wear this every day. Don't take it off until I ask you to return it."

"Why?" I ask, my voice small and whiny, like a two-year-old who doesn't want to eat her broccoli.

"It's the only way I'll know what's happening to you. Please," she says, taking my hands and looking at me intently. "Please trust me."

I swallow the knot in my throat and nod.

What choice do I have?

Twenty-One

Three Dannabelle Grimm books cover the space between me and Kendall.

I've read each one, but I haven't done any of the work. For once I'm determined to stand up to Kendall and make her do her fair share.

"Have you done the reading?" I ask. I'm careful to keep my left hand in my lap so as to avoid any questioning about the bracelet. Like I don't have enough questions of my own. Has Lady Rose bugged the bracelet with some kind of camera and microphone?

Kendall gives me a look. "What do you think?"

"I think I hope you've read it or we'll never get the project finished."

"I've read enough."

I tilt my head to the side. I'm not sure if it's the amulet or the bracelet or my total lack of common sense that makes me challenge her.

"When was Dannabelle Grimm the High Priestess?"

Kendall crosses her arms over her chest, like she's too good to answer.

"From 1845 to 1851. How did she die?"

More death glares shoot through me.

"Pneumonia. What was her gift?"

Kendall sighs deeply. "Why don't you tell me?"

"Inheritance. That means she could inherit gifts from other witches just by touching something they owned."

Kendall shrugs, but the stubborn shield around her seems to crumble just a little.

"Look, Kendall. I know we'll never be friends. I'm okay with that. But my grade is riding on you doing your part. Let's just get the work done, get it over with, and go back to ignoring each other."

Hearing the words come from my lips is like a liberating out-of-body experience. I am getting used to standing up to Kendall.

I look at the bracelet Lady Rose gave me, then back at Kendall's defeated face. Did Lady Rose's bracelet obliterate my fear of Kendall? Did she give me a power?

Kendall opens her spiral, then grabs the smallest Dannabelle Grimm book from the pile, completely unaware of what's going on. Somehow I have absorbed fearlessness from a bracelet.

Without looking up at me, Kendall says, "Let's start the outline."

Most nights, Ivy hangs out in my room and Kendall hangs out in Ivy's with Zena. Unlike most nights, when we study and chat, tonight I watch Ivy get ready for the social, and grow more and more impatient with each outfit change.

She tries on her third outfit—a pair of jeans with bling on the pockets, and a white shirt with a cute little ruffle on the bottom. The zebra-striped flats on her feet add just the right touch.

Ivy looks at herself in the mirror, twisting around to see her backside. "This is the one. Right? I don't know. What do you think? Is this the one?"

With our perfect hair and complexions still intact, what we wear isn't as important as it used to be. "I like it," I tell her.

She turns to face me, hands on hips. Her gorgeous curly red hair frames her frustration.

"That's what you said about the other two."

"I like all three of them."

"Which one do you like the best? You have to have a favorite."

I stifle an eye roll. Ivy is way too happy with our new-found popularity. "Fine. I like this one the best."

"Me too," she says with a smile. She rubs her hands together. "Now, what are you going to wear?"

"Haven't even thought about it," I confess.

"What in the world is wrong with you?" Ivy marches to my dresser, opens the drawers, and begins pulling out clothes and laying them on the bed.

"What's wrong with *you*?" I ask. "Have you forgotten that until Kendall's spell went wrong, we were as invisible as air? Who cares what people think? I didn't care before, and I don't care now."

She shakes her head like I'm a lost cause. Maybe there is something wrong with me. "It's a dance," she says, pairing pants with shirts and shoes. "With *boys*."

"Who are witches. Or wizards."

"Even cooler."

"You realize we won't be able to talk with them after we leave the dance, right? We have no cell phones, no email, nothing."

"But there's always next year," she says with a sly grin.

I can't help but laugh.

"What do you think?" she asks.

I look at the outfits on the bed. They're all pretty boring. Before my transformation nobody noticed me, so it didn't matter what I wore. But Ivy's excitement is contagious and I find myself caring. About *clothes*.

"You pick," I tell her. Ivy's fashion sense beats mine by a country mile, so I'm happy to let her be the boss.

She analyzes the clothes, murmuring to herself quietly, switching tops and shoes around.

I look at the clock. 5:40. "Twenty minutes," I remind her.

"Okay. This one." She points to the first outfit, which is a pair of denim capris with little worn spots on them. My mom bought them for me, but I refused to wear them to school. Even if everyone else was wearing them, I wasn't going to. That would only have made me look like a wannabe, and Kendall would have teased me endlessly. Now I'm glad I packed them, because Ivy's right. They're perfect for tonight.

The top is a simple bright pink short-sleeve shirt, the hem lined with rhinestones. It's just dressy enough.

"Good choice," I tell her.

I slip the clothes on, and when I look at myself, I feel more confident than I ever have. I run my fingers through my hair and let it fall naturally, still amazed that it looks so perfect.

Ivy claps her hands. "Ooh! I've got just the thing for your hair."

She runs out the door and is back in less than a minute. In her hand is a multicolored polka-dot scarf. She puts it on my head like a headband and ties it under my hair. The long ends of the colorful scarf fall over my shoulder to my waist. She stands back, looks at me thoughtfully, then nods. "Perfect."

I turn back to the mirror to look at my reflection.

I hardly recognize the girl in the mirror. I look more like the Crafters that walk the halls, with their impeccable good looks. I don't know what Kendall did wrong in her spell, but I'm actually thankful she did it.

"Shoes?" I ask Ivy.

She looks at my choices. Black ballet flats, tennis shoes, and silver glitter Keds.

"Keds."

I put the shoes on, then look at the clock. " Let's get Jo and Dru."

"Wait," Ivy says. "What about the amulet?"

I look at the pillow, where the amulet is hidden deep inside the stuffing.

"It'll show," I tell her. "But . . ."

"You're not going to need it tonight," Ivy says. "Tonight we're just girls. Not witches."

I think for a moment, then look down at the bracelet on my wrist.

"You're right. I don't need the amulet tonight."

We walk out of the room, and I take one last look at my pillow and pray I'm doing the right thing by leaving the amulet here. With a snap of my fingers, the door closes, and we walk to Dru and Jo's room.

It takes a full minute before Jo opens the door. And when she does, I'm speechless. Her hair is in perfect curls around her face, and her bangs are pulled back with a pretty rhinestone clip. Her face turns red when we gawk at her, openmouthed.

"Quit staring, weirdos." She walks away from the door, and we follow her inside, unable to take our eyes off her. She's wearing jeans and a green shirt with puffy see-through sleeves.

"Jo," Ivy says. "You look freaking awesome!"

Jo gives us a weak eye roll, but you can tell she's pleased. I bet Jo's life back home was a lot like mine, where the less you stood out, the less you got picked on, where blending into the walls was a good thing.

"How'd you get your hair so curly?" I ask. "It's almost as curly as Ivy's."

Dru pops out of the bathroom in a perky bright red sundress. "With this," she says, holding up a curling iron.

"Where and how did you get that? Did you sneak it in?"

"Welllllll . . . ," she says, looking at Jo before saying anything else.

"Well, what?" Ivy asks.

"It's my gift," Dru says.

"What's your gift? Hairstyling?"

Dru slaps me playfully on my shoulder. "No, dummy. I have the gift of conjuration."

"Say what?" Ivy asks.

"Conjuration," Dru repeats. "It means I can make things appear. We needed a curling iron, and bibbity-bobbity-boo, here it is."

"No way!" Ivy's wide eyes are looking at the curling iron, then back at Dru, then back at the curling iron. "Do it again."

"I'm not a circus act," Dru says. But the smile on her face shows how happy she is. And I'm happy for her. Conjuration is a very cool gift.

Jo's face lights up. "Conjure up some lip gloss."

Dru shakes her head. "We aren't allowed to wear lip gloss."

"Make it clear," I say. "That way we can say it's ChapStick."

Dru thinks about it briefly, then shrugs. "What could it hurt?"

She closes her eyes and whispers words I can't hear. There's a crackling in the air that feels like static electricity, then *bam*! Lip gloss is in her hand.

"Omigosh! That's so flipping cool!" I say, practically screaming. "You're so lucky!"

Dru laughs and passes the lip gloss to me. "Your wish is my command."

"Let's go," I say. "We're supposed to be in the lobby in two minutes."

Ivy stops at the door before opening it. "I really wish we had a camera. This is going to be a great night."

For the first time since the social was announced, I actually believe her.

Twenty-Two

We stand in front of Dowling around a tree that almost completely hides the building. The lazy branches stretch across the lawn, extending from one side of the Dowling driveway to the other. I stand with other well-dressed Seekers inside the safety of those branches. There's something magical, and totally creepy, about standing in a circle under the thick canopy of foliage, the tree's leaves rustling despite the still air.

The headmistress stands in the center of our circle, a black velvet cape draped over her head and brushing the grass. She holds a long white candle in her hand, its flame our only light. As it flickers, it feels like every leaf has a set of eyes, watching us beneath this tree.

"Girls, before you head out, there is a special travel

spell that I hope will help you on your journey."

In the clear and commanding voice that defines our headmistress, she speaks.

"Seekers, may you be blessed.
May all good things come to you,
may nothing whatsoever harm you,
may your heart be light,
may your travels be safe,
may your health be good,
may your mind be sound,
may your friendships sustain you,
may you be blessed in every way,
and may you return home safely."

Home.

I never thought I'd call Dowling home, but I guess that's what it has become. How many other girls have stood beneath this tree's branches? Hundreds? Thousands? Dannabelle stood here. So did my great-great-grandmother. And I suddenly feel the sisterhood the headmistress was talking about. It's about more than just me. It's about the girls who've been here before and the girls who have yet to come, and being connected to all of them.

I reach for the amulet and remember I've left it in my room. I should've brought it. Even if it meant wearing something hideous, I should have found a way to hide it.

Before I can run back to the room and get it, Ivy grabs my hand and drags me to the chartered bus, talking non-stop about boys and dancing and boys, boys, boys! We haven't even left Dowling, and Ivy's already obsessed with the boys we haven't met yet.

The last two girls to walk onto the bus are Kendall and Zena. My entire body stiffens in frustration when I see what they're wearing. Compared to the rest of the girls on the bus, Kendall and Zena look like they're headed to a Hollywood movie opening, not a dance for sixth graders.

Zena is dressed in a black dress covered in sequins. She's wearing heels, and her normally curly hair is beautifully straightened.

Kendall's emerald-green dress sits off her shoulders, and the fabric falls softly over her arms. Her blond hair virtually blinds me with its shininess.

The pair walks with cool sophistication to empty seats

behind me and Ivy. You can practically see every girl's shoulders sag as Zena and Kendall pass them, their own confidence deflated by the sight of the two. Even *I* shrink a little as they pass me, and I don't care about impressing the boys at the dance.

"There goes our chance to impress anyone at Riley," Ivy mutters.

I shake my head. "Don't give it a second thought. The boys won't be able to ignore you. I mean, seriously. Have you seen your hair?"

Ivy leans back in her seat, a small smile on her face, but the spark in her eyes is gone. We ride in silence, watching the world pass by. It feels odd to be outside the Dowling walls after spending so many weeks there. I almost forgot there *is* life outside the black iron gates.

It isn't until the bus slows and turns into the Riley driveway that Ivy begins talking nervously.

"I hope they play good music. Not a bunch of old stuff. And I hope there's just the right amount of slow songs. Not too many, but a few would be nice. Think they'll have snacks? I'm hungry."

When we step off the bus, she stops talking and admires the building in front of us. Riley is much bigger than Dowling, standing twelve or thirteen stories high with dark red brick, and windows trimmed with black shutters.

The boys wait to greet us, stretched in long lines on either side of the door. A dorm mom I don't know snaps her fingers, and we follow her instinctively. I wish Miss A was here, but she left town for the weekend, leaving another dorm mom to escort us. Miss A always knows how to make everyone comfortable. We walk awkwardly to the door, sneaking sideways glances at the boys, either too afraid or too embarrassed to make actual eye contact. Most of the girls are the picture of excitement, but all I feel is a sense of dread. This is going to be the longest two hours of my life.

Once inside we're ushered to a room elaborately decorated for tonight's event. The almost-black wood that lines the walls is lit by a ton of candles, and white streamers drape across the ceiling. I try to ignore the obvious fire hazard and just enjoy the beauty of the room. Like the Gathering Circle at Dowling, it's the kind of room that commands your respect.

One of my favorite Maroon 5 songs pumps through the speakers, and Ivy half-walks, half-dances her way to the snack table. Pizza, cheese, and crackers fill a long table, and delicious sodas are shoved in tubs of ice. I totally thought there would be better snacks. I mean, come on. We're *witches*. Despite the lame spread, my mouth waters at the thought of drinking a Dr Pepper, and I get in line with Ivy to grab one.

The boys enter the room, and the sounds of happy girl voices fall silent. Following their own adult leader, the boys join us at the snack table and ask if they can help us. Their politeness is awkward, and no one really responds. We just smile, grab our food and drinks, and race to the nearest table.

When the boys fail to ask anyone to dance after three songs, some of the girls decide to dance with each other. Kendall and Zena don't, of course. They already have a circle of adoring fans. Ivy nudges me with her elbow. "Don't look now, but there's a guy staring at you."

"Uh-huh. I'm sure he's looking at someone else."

Dru shakes her head. "No, she's telling the truth. He's standing at Kendall's table, and she's talking to him, but he's staring at you."

I laugh out loud. "Riiiiiight." I've spent my entire life in Kendall's shadow. That isn't about to change now.

"Look for yourself," Jo says, her bright blue eyes shining.

Just to shut them up, I turn and look back at Kendall's table.

My heart hammers double time when I see him. His light brown hair lies just above his eyebrows, and his eyes are focused on me. Even while Kendall touches his arm and tosses her hair, he looks only at me. I look away self-consciously. "Stalk much?" I mutter.

"He's so cute, Hallie," Ivy says. "Don't be dense. Smile at him."

There's a part of me that would love nothing more than to steal Kendall's thunder. But the sane, reasonable part of me knows better. Encouraging this boy with a smile while he's talking to Kendall would be like poking a rabid dog.

Dru slaps her hand over her mouth. "Omigosh."

"He's dancing with Kendall?" I ask.

She shakes her head several times.

Ivy grabs my arm and squeezes. "He's coming over here."

Jo laughs, watching the scene unfold. "You should see Kendall. If looks could kill . . . well, you'd be a pile of ashes."

No, no, no, no, no.

Please don't come over here, please don't come over here.

My eyes are closed and I'm repeating the words in my head, when I hear him clear his throat.

Why didn't he turn around? He's supposed to do what I think!

I open my eyes and find every girl at my table staring at the boy, wide-eyed. Up close I can see he's got light brown eyes, and his smile belongs in a toothpaste commercial. Dressed in jeans and an untucked button-down shirt, he is as close to perfect as I've ever seen. He isn't just the normal cute like Jasper Williams back home. He's got a great smile and oozes confidence.

"Hi," he says, extending his hand. "I'm Cody Ray."

I stare at his hand for five long seconds before shaking it. My heart flutters faster than a hummingbird's wings when I touch him.

"Hi," I say, my voice more squeak than anything else. Isn't *he* the one who's supposed to have a squeaky voice?

"She's Hallie. Hallie Simon," Ivy says, jumping in to save me. "I'm Ivy, and this is Dru and Jo."

Cody smiles and says hello to them, then turns his attention back to me.

"Want to dance?" he asks, his face turning just the lightest shade of pink. I can't say no. He's too cute to say no to.

I don't look at Kendall before I answer him. "Sure."

I stand from the table and follow him to the dance floor, grateful the Black Eyed Peas are playing. But just as we reach the floor, the song fades. He looks at me and grins, and I positively melt. I thought going weak in the knees was an overused cliché, but it actually happens.

When the next song begins, I freeze. It's not another fast song we can dance to standing three feet from each other. It's a slow song, something that will require us to actually touch. I look back at my table, at the safety net of my friends, and their insistent expressions tell me to suck it up and dance with him.

I take another deep breath.

It's just a boy. You won't even see him again until next year's social. Relax.

He holds out his hand, and I take it. I'm grateful he doesn't pull me too close, leaving plenty of room between us. We're the only two people on the floor, and it's impossible to ignore every single person in the room watching us.

"So how do you like Dowling?" he asks.

He wants to talk?

I carefully follow his choppy footsteps, praying I don't step on his feet. Why wasn't that in tonight's blessing?

"It's good," I say. "Different than I expected."

I wonder if these boys go through the same things we do.

He laughs. "I know what you mean."

I feel my body relax a little, and a rush of questions pop into my head.

How long have you lived at Riley?

Do you have gifts like us?

What's your family history with witchcraft?

Why'd you pick me over Kendall?

I don't remember all the rules for tonight's dance, because I didn't think I'd be doing anything more than sitting and watching. Are we allowed to talk about magic? About our gifts?

"Are those your roommates?" he asks. "At the table?"

"No, they're just my friends. My roommate is Kendall."

He looks at me blankly. "Who's that?"

My feet stop, and he steps on my toes.

"Sorry," he says, face red.

I focus on my feet, then answer. "Kendall's the girl you were talking to before you came to my table."

"Oh," he says, a weird look on his face. "You don't seem like you'd be roommates."

"I know. We don't get to pick until next year."

"At least you just have one roommate. We have four boys to a room. Bunk beds. It's like living at summer camp."

I giggle at his description. I suspect his room is much nicer than anything at summer camp. "I'd kill to have more people in our room."

"Really?"

I nod. "Yeah. At least then I'd have someone to talk to."

His face cringes. "That bad, huh?"

"Yep."

The song fades, and a fast song blares through the speakers. The dance floor begins crowding with kids, some dancing together, some dancing in groups, some dancing alone.

Cody and I continue dancing together. I thought I'd be grateful for the loud music so we wouldn't have to talk, but instead I'm disappointed. He's easy to talk to, and I know he'll be a good friend. Assuming I ever see him again.

Kendall and Zena are on the dance floor all night, dancing with different boys each time. It's like they're taste-testing at an ice cream factory. Cody and I dance most of the night, stopping only to eat and drink.

It seems like minutes, but it must have been two hours,

because the lights in the room brighten and the music stops.

I look around for my friends, who have been dancing with each other. They're waving at me, walking back to the table for a last swallow of their drinks.

"Well," I say. "I had fun."

And I did. I can't believe how much fun I had, actually.

"Me too," he says, smiling. "So, I know you can't really talk at Dowling."

I nod, sad that I can't talk to him anytime I want.

"But we'll see each other at the summer solstice celebration."

I don't have a clue what he's talking about, but I smile anyway. "Sounds great."

I look back at my friends, then turn back to Cody. Do we hug? Shake hands? Should I just walk away?

Before I can think about it too much, he grabs me for a quick hug. My arms stay limp at my sides, and I'm worried I might pass out because I've quit breathing.

"Bye, Hallie," he says. Butterflies beat inside my stomach as I watch him walk to his waiting friends.

I prepare myself for the barrage of questions that are coming. But for the next few seconds, before I get to Ivy, I let myself accept that boys aren't so bad after all.

*   *   *   *   *

When I finally crawl into bed an hour later, I'm so tired, I can barely keep my eyes open. Kendall's bed is still made and she isn't in the bathroom, but I'm too exhausted to care about where she is or what she's doing. She did a nice job of glaring at me the entire bus ride home. I didn't have to look behind me to know it; it was like two torches burning my back.

When we were working on our research project in history this morning, I saw a glimmer of the old Kendall. The one I knew before third grade. The one who cared about me. That all changed when Cody asked me to dance. But as much as I don't want Kendall on my bad side any more than normal, I don't regret dancing with Cody. He was a surprise . . . different than other boys I've known. Not once did he make a farting noise or say something gross. He didn't act like he was better than anyone else, and he was nice to everyone.

I remember the amulet and reach inside my pillowcase. Relief washes over me when I feel its familiar warmth. I pull it over my head and tuck it inside my pajama shirt.

I can't keep the amulet. I know I can't. But I'm not quite ready to let it go. I don't know how much power it's giving me. I only know how it makes me feel. More confident. Less frightened.

Tonight was almost perfect. The only thing that marred it was Kendall's resentment.

If I have the power of mind manipulation, maybe I can change how she feels about me. Maybe I can make her go back to the way she was, to the *real* Kendall. I think it'll take more than some sixth-grade spell to change her, but it's worth a try. Anything is better than living with someone who hates me.

With my mind focused on Kendall, I say my wish for her.

"May Kendall's true spirit be shown from this day forward.

"May Kendall's true spirit be shown from this day forward.

"May Kendall's true spirit be shown from this day forward."

I am too tired to read, too tired to journal. I turn off the light and sleep.

Twenty-Three

When my alarm goes off the following morning, I'm barely able to move my arms. I can't believe I'm actually sore from dancing. Maybe I should spend some of my Personal Growth time exercising.

I look at the bed across from me and see Kendall still sleeping. I fight the urge to wake her up and see if my spell worked. Half-afraid of what I'll find, I decide against it and pull myself out of bed, each step I take more painful than the next. By the time I get to the bathroom, I'm out of breath and every bone and organ and cell inside me is screaming.

I know something isn't right. I'm sick. Really sick. Did Cody get me sick? He seemed fine yesterday. In fact, I don't remember anyone being sick yesterday.

I reach into the shower to turn the water on, but before I can touch the knob, I'm drowning in a sea of black stars.

Ivy is standing over me when I open my eyes. Her green eyes are darker than normal, worried. The brightness in the room burns my eyes, so I close them again.

"Hallie, wake up," she says, slapping my hand. "Wake up."

I squint my eyes open to prove I'm not sleeping. "I'm awake, but the light . . ."

I hear her click off my lamp. "There. Is that better?"

I open my eyes wider and nod. "What happened?"

She leans over and talks quietly into my ear. "Kendall found you face down in the shower."

The memory of the morning comes back to me. "I passed out."

"Well, duh. You're sicker than sick. You've been knocked out for an hour."

I attempt to turn onto my side, but it hurts too much. "Why am I so sore?"

Ivy doesn't answer but leans close to me again, whispering, "Where's the amulet?"

I put my hand on my stomach, then around my neck. I

stick my hand inside my pillow, feeling for the hard amulet in the stuffing. But nothing's there.

It's gone.

Pure panic washes over me like a bucket of ice-cold water.

I look at Ivy, and we both know Kendall must have taken it.

I close my eyes again. "I'm going to be in so much trouble."

The door to my room opens, and Ivy leans back quickly. "She's awake," she says to someone I can't see.

A woman in a gauzy green dress comes closer and puts her hand to my forehead. "You're still running a heck of a fever," she says. "I can't remember the last time someone was this sick at Dowling."

She puts something into my hand, clasps her hands tight around mine, and whispers words I can't hear.

I close my eyes, too tired to keep them open, and fall back asleep to the woman's inaudible chanting.

The next time I wake up, Ivy is lying in bed with me. It must be nighttime, because the room is pitch black. I try to move, to sit up in bed, but I'm too weak to do it alone. Honest-to-Saffra fear shoots through me. What kind of disease did Cody give me? Maybe he and Kendall were working together all along, plotting my fate. And I thought he was one of the nice boys.

"Ivy," I whisper. I hardly recognize my own voice. It's so quiet, I can barely hear myself.

Ivy doesn't budge. I take a breath and try again. "Ivy."

She jerks away, nearly tossing me off the bed. "You're awake!"

She reaches across me and clicks the light on.

"What's wrong with me?" I ask her.

Ivy shakes her head. "No one knows. One of the best hedge witches at Dowling has been taking care of you, but she can't figure it out. They've called for Miss A to come back early."

I wonder if they've called my mom. I'm so homesick, I could cry. Mom always knows how to make me feel better, and Dad can make me laugh no matter how sick I am.

The image of Miss A makes me smile. She may not be my mother, but I always feel safe and protected around her. "When will she be here?" I ask.

Ivy shrugs. "Not sure. They said sometime tomorrow."

"You shouldn't be in bed with me. You shouldn't even be in my room."

"Uh-huh. Right. I'll just leave you here to be miserable alone. Would you do that to me?"

I shake my head. "No, but . . ."

"Stop talking before you make me mad. I'm here. Get over it."

I smile at Ivy, so thankful we found each other. "Where's Kendall?"

"Since I refused to go back to my room, they moved her to my room until you're better. Kendall was totally freaking out and wouldn't talk. She just pointed at the bathroom, and that's how I knew you were in there."

"I can't believe she hates me so much, she wouldn't even help me."

"She and Zena deserve each other."

"Does she have the amulet? We have to get it back," I say.

Ivy's face changes. I already know the answer before she speaks. "I didn't ask her."

I close my eyes, avoiding the reality of how much trouble I'm going to be in. "She hasn't always been this way."

Ivy puts a cool rag that smells of mint on my forehead. "Shh. Sleep."

Eyes already closed, I quickly fall back into the safe, warm peace of darkness.

✳   ✳   ✳   ✳   ✳

The next time I wake up, Miss A is sitting in the desk chair and Ivy is sitting on the foot of my bed.

"Look who decided to wakey-wakey!" Miss A's happy voice makes me grin.

"See what happens when you leave?" I tease her.

She puts a hand to her chest. "It's the curse of being so wonderful."

Ivy and I both giggle. For the first time in two days, I feel like I can actually move without screaming in pain.

"I feel like I've been beat up. Everything hurts."

Miss A opens a bronze case and piddles with something I can't see. "I know, sugar. Just hang in there. It'll get better, I promise."

"What are you doing?" I ask her.

"Fixing you," she says. "Which, let me tell you, is no small task. This one was a humdinger!"

"I must have gotten it at the dance," I say.

She sprinkles something onto my head, then places a cold rag over it.

"Speaking of the dance," she says, "I heard you danced all night."

I look at Ivy, and she holds up her hands. "I didn't say a thing."

"Hallie. When are you going to realize there are no secrets at Dowling?"

I feel my face warming in embarrassment.

"Speaking of secrets . . . ," she begins.

Dread curls around my spine. I look at Ivy, whose face is paler than normal. I feel the absence of the amulet against my skin and know Miss A knows.

"Of course I know," she says softly. "I've known since the day you took it."

I stare at Miss A, speechless.

"You surprised me. I never dreamed you'd hang on to it so long."

I take a deep breath and begin my worthless explanation. "I know I should've told you right away. But it made me feel stronger. And then I couldn't figure out how to get it back into the case without anyone knowing, and I—"

Miss A puts a chubby finger to my lips to quiet me. "I know, Hallie."

"Then why didn't you say anything?"

"Because you had to discover your gift on your own. That's your main purpose as a Seeker."

I look at her, then at Ivy. "But the amulet doesn't have anything to do with my gift."

Miss A just looks at me, all joking gone, face serious.

"Wait. It does? How?"

"When you came to Dowling, what did you think your gift would be?" she asks me.

"I thought I'd be a hedge witch like my great-great-grandmother."

"Guess what?" she says with a wink. "That's my gift. Not yours."

I put my hand on the wet rag lying on my forehead. Miss A? A hedge witch?

"Lady Rose said I have the gift of mind manipulation."

Miss A nods, her curls bouncing. "You do."

"But then I was able to become invisible."

She takes my arm and rubs the inside of my wrists with something, leaving dark green smudges. She wipes her hands on a rag in her lap, then closes the lid to her container.

Is she deliberately not answering me?

She gives me a look. "No, I'm not deliberately ignoring you."

I give her a wide-eyed look. My body aches for answers. How do people know what I'm thinking?

Miss A chuckles, and I feel myself relax. "I can read every thought in your head, silly girl. So can the headmistress. You've known that for a while. You just didn't want to admit it to yourself. It's part of the mind manipulation gift. You just haven't learned how to close your mind off to others."

"Does she have more than one gift?" Ivy asks. "Because I swear to you, she disappeared. Right here on this bed."

Miss A nods. "I believe you."

"So?" I ask. "What's my gift?"

"Your gift," Miss A says, "is the gift of inheritance."

I rack my brains trying to remember what that gift is. I know I've heard about it before. Was it Dannabelle?

"Yes, Dannabelle had it."

"What does it mean?" Ivy asks.

"It's really rare. I've never known a witch with that gift."

"Just tell me!" I say.

"The gift of inheritance means you can absorb the gift of other witches if you touch something that was theirs. Saffra's amulet gave you the gift of mind manipulation. The broach Lady Rose asked you to hold gave you the gift of invisibility."

I touch the bracelet still on my wrist. Lady Rose was testing my gift. "What gift does this give me?"

"Transformation."

"I don't understand."

"It means you can change physically something about a person," she says.

I shrug, then take the bracelet off. "Well, it must not work, because nothing like that has happened."

Miss A takes the bracelet with a small smile. "We'll see."

"Miss A," I say, terrified to say any more. But I know I have to come clean. "I lost the amulet. I think Kendall has it."

"The amulet is safe," she says. Her face is calm and untroubled, and I let my body relax.

"So now what?" I ask, shifting in my bed to get more comfortable.

"Well, there's one more thing you need to know, Hallie." Miss A looks at Ivy.

"You can say anything in front of her," I tell her.

Miss A nods, then takes my hands in hers. My empty stomach clenches in dread.

"The gift of inheritance is incredibly powerful. It's not a . . . *normal* gift."

"I knew it," I say. "I knew there was something wrong with me."

"Sugar, that's not what I mean. The gift of inheritance is a dark magic gift."

"Wait just a minute," Ivy says, holding up her hands. "Isn't that forbidden?"

"Well, normally, yes. But some witches, very rare witches, are born to be . . . special. Like you, Hallie."

"I don't want to be a dark magic witch," I tell her. "Can I change it?"

Miss A shrugs. "You can't change who you were meant to be. Generally speaking, the spells you cast are going to have negative results. That doesn't mean you can't train yourself to learn good magic too. It'll just be harder for you."

I feel sick. I should never have allowed myself to think I could start fresh. It doesn't matter where I go, I'll always stand out. And not in a good way, not in the way I want. I think back on the wishes I've made, how they've never really had the results I wanted.

"No matter what I tried to do, everything I wished for came out horrible."

"Exactly. That's the dark magic part of your gift."

I close my eyes and try to imagine myself as a dark witch. I can't believe I was born to be *this*.

"You want to hear the funny thing?" Miss A says secretly.

"Please," I beg.

"Your roomie? Kendall? She has the gift of transformation as well. But she isn't a dark witch, so her transformations are good, even when her intentions are not. You can thank her for your makeovers."

The irony that Kendall made us pretty is still funny.

Ivy and I both smile, then burst out laughing. Even Miss A laughs with us. And I have a feeling everything might just be okay after all.

Twenty-Four

Two days later I'm back to normal.

Well, no, that's not entirely true. Everyone in the building now knows I'm the first dark witch since Dannabelle. Like her, I intend to make my gift as useful as I can. And when the occasional spell goes wrong, well, I'll just smile through it like Dannabelle did.

It's impossible to believe I'm going to be as powerful as Dannabelle, that even Kendall can't surpass my abilities.

I still miss the weight of the amulet around my neck. It seems so out of place back in the library case.

Kendall hasn't spoken a word to me since the night of the dance, which is rude even for her. You'd think she'd at least fake giving a flip about me being so sick.

But today is different.

When I wake up, Kendall is sitting up in bed, fully dressed, watching me sleep. I scream when I see her staring at me.

"Omigod," I yell. "Are you trying to kill me?"

She gives me a small grin, and I worry that I might be right.

"You know, Kendall, I'm really tired of the games. I'm tired of trying to get you to like me. I'm tired of trying to help you and getting pushed away. I'm just tired of all of it. You win. We won't be friends. I'm okay with that."

I swing my legs to the floor and stand up.

Kendall holds up a hand to stop me.

"What? What could you possibly want with me, Kendall?"

A sad look streaks across her face. She motions for me to sit next to her.

My feet don't move, sensing a trap.

"I won't bite," she says, rolling her eyes. I perch myself on the edge of her bed, ready to spring out of the way if she tries anything funny.

I don't say anything, just wait for her to spew whatever venom is coming.

"I know how you got sick," she says quietly.

"What are you talking about?" I ask.

"That night. The night of the dance."

"What about it?"

"I was really mad when we came back."

"About?" I ask, like I don't know it's about Cody.

She gives me the look again. "What do you think, Hallie? Jeez, you can be so irritating."

I stand to go to the bathroom.

She grabs my arm, and I look at her with all the anger inside me. "Let go of me."

She drops her hand to her lap. "Let me finish."

I cross my arms but stay standing. I'm not sure where this is going, but I don't have to be psychic to know it's bad.

"So Zena . . . well, she put a spell on you for me."

I stare at Kendall in disbelief. "You aren't serious. You made me sick? *On purpose?*"

She nods, head down. "I knew that any spell I put on you would backfire. Everything I tried to do to set you back only made you more popular, more beautiful, because of my gift of transformation for good. So I asked Zena to do it for me, thinking that, if I didn't participate in casting the spell, it might actually work."

"What kind of spell did she use?"

Because I might just put it on her! I don't care whose daughter she is.

"It was a hex, really. I never dreamed it'd make you so sick."

I consider calling Miss A, telling someone about this before Zena actually kills me. But I have to handle Kendall on my own. For once. "It's one thing to not like me, but to actually hurt me? That's low, Kendall. Even for you."

"I didn't mean for it to be so bad. I just wanted you to . . . I don't know."

I look at Kendall. She looks the same on the outside, but something's different. Maybe it's just how I feel about her that has changed. I actually feel pity for her.

"Why are you telling me this? You know I could get you into a lot of trouble."

She shrugs. "I don't know."

"Know what's really pathetic? While you were trying to hurt me, I was trying to help you."

Kendall looks shocked. "What?"

"I just wanted the real you to be shown. I remember the real you—the one who laughed at my stupid jokes, the one who always defended me. That's who I wished you'd become.

The *real* Kendall. Not this monster you've turned into."

Kendall's eyes fill with tears, and I nearly panic. I have *never* seen her cry. Not even when the dodgeball hit her in the face in fourth grade.

"When?" she asks forcefully.

"When what?"

"When did you put that spell on me?"

"The night of the dance. I said it right before I went to sleep. Probably about the same time you were trying to kill me."

She takes a deep breath. "I'm going to show you something, but you have to stay calm. I'm already scared enough for both of us. Don't. Freak. Out."

Every cell in my body does the Jell-O jiggle.

I cross my arms over my chest in a show of fake bravado. Like nothing she could show me would surprise me.

She opens her mouth and sticks out her tongue.

Her *forked* tongue.

As in her look-at-me-I'm-a-snake tongue. I stare at it in shock and fight the urge to run from the room.

I hear Miss A's voice in my head telling me I have the gift of transformation. This can't be happening. There's no way this is real.

"What *is* that?" I ask, doing my best to keep the disgust from my voice.

Kendall closes her mouth, wipes tears from her face. "You should know. You did it to me."

"I don't get it," I tell her.

"Come on, Hallie. Don't be stupid. When you cast the spell for the real me to be shown, this is what happened." She points at her tongue.

My mind is reeling. I wanted the real Kendall to be shown, and she gets a snake tongue? The *real* Kendall . . . is a snake. I fight dueling emotions of pity and victory.

"That's what this is about. You want me to reverse it," I say.

She doesn't confirm my suspicions but stays silent.

"Look, Kendall, I don't even know how to reverse it. You know how my magic works. I would probably just make it worse.

She looks at me with a mixture of regret, anger, and fear. Despite my determination to hate her as thoroughly as possible, a tiny little part of me feels bad for her.

"You can change," I tell her. "Heck, you're a good witch. Anything's possible."

"Maybe," she says.

I glance at the clock. "I have to get in the shower or I'm going to be late."

Kendall nods. Just as I reach the bathroom door, she asks, "Are you going to tell Miss A?"

I look at Kendall, at the girl I wanted as my best friend. I think about Ivy and how she never left me the entire time I was sick.

"Nah," I tell her with a smile. "I think I came out on top this time."

I close the door to the bathroom and look at myself in the mirror. Despite being sick, despite being so afraid of my gift, I'm happy.

I'm gifted with special powers and unbelievable friends.

I'm a Seeker at Dowling and will one day be a witch.

If you ask me, this is the mother of all do-overs. And this is just the beginning.

Read on for a sneak peek of
the companion to
The XYZs of Being Wicked.

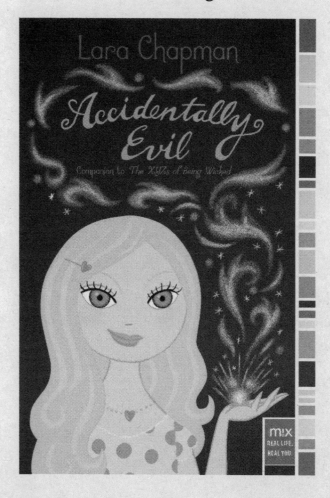

Unless you've been blessed with the gift of premonition, there's no preparing for your second first day at Dowling.

Last year I entered the Dowling Academy School of Witchcraft in fear, all sweaty hands and pounding heart.

Last year I hauled my impossibly heavy trunk to my room. Last year everything—and I mean *everything*—changed.

I walk under the large oak tree, now fully aware of what happens beneath it. Blessings and socials, and darker things I've yet to see, I'm sure. My senses, dulled by the scorching Texas heat and never-ending summer days, zap to life.

There's a bounce in my step as I keep myself from

running inside to find my best friend, Ivy. It's been two long months since I've seen her. FaceTime just isn't the same as being with someone. Plus it was impossible to talk about boys or magic or gossip without one of our mothers eavesdropping. So we had to settle for late-night texting to talk about the good stuff.

I pat the iPhone in my back pocket, happy I'm allowed to have it. Last year I was a Seeker, which means I was a beginner. Seekers have almost no privileges. No phones, no television, no computers. It was a lot like prison, but with better food.

Since this is my second year, I'm a Crafter, which means I know what my gift is (that's a really long story) and I've passed the Seeker exam. I'm a long way from being a real witch, though. That takes years.

I stop in front of the massive Dowling doors that once seemed so forbidding. Just me. No parents. No trunk. *No nerves.*

What a difference a year makes.

I pull the door open and let the cool air wash over me. Before I'm fully inside the building, I hear Miss A call my name.

"Hallie!"

My eyes adjust to the dim lighting, and my dorm mom's face becomes clear. I break into a huge smile. Last year I accidentally made her dye her hair orange, and she hasn't changed it since. Beneath that tangled curly mess of shocking hair is the face I've missed so much. She was only my dorm mom for a year, but we have a special connection.

She pulls me into a big squishy hug. "Looky here, looky here! Aren't you a sight for sore eyes!"

I laugh and pull out of the embrace. "I missed you, too, Miss A."

I've tried to forget that Miss A won't be my dorm mom this year. All the other dorm moms are über-serious and a little bit scary. Miss A's like the crazy grandmother at family reunions. Her face is painted too bright and her lipstick is always smeared across her teeth. But you just know she's always going to be there for you.

"Is Ivy here yet?" I ask.

She checks her watch before answering. "Her mama called and said they were running late. Should be here in about an hour."

I try not to look too disappointed. I'm excited about seeing Miss A, but Ivy is the one I really want to see. When you go through what we have so far, you're more than just friends. You're sisters.

I glance at the staircase and smile. "Our trunks are here."

"You betcha," Miss A says, smiling.

The trunks whiz up the stairs, two feet off the ground, unassisted. When we witnessed it last year, Ivy passed out. She would've hit the floor and split her head open if Miss A hadn't frozen her midfall. Magic saved the day—something that would happen many times after.

"Didn't I tell you this would happen for you as a Crafter?" Miss A asks.

"You did." I am mesmerized by the trunks and wonder if mine's been delivered to my room.

"It's already in there," Miss A answers.

It takes me a second to remember that my thoughts project. No one had heard my thoughts all summer. I kind of liked it that way.

"If you don't want me reading your thoughts, you'd better get busy figuring out how to close that brain of yours off from me," she says with a wink. "And everyone else."

"Yes, ma'am," I answer. There are a lot of things I still don't understand about my gift. Or gifts. With the gift of inheritance, I can acquire gifts from other witches. For instance, I accidentally picked up the gift of mind manipulation. That means sometimes people hear my thoughts about what I think they should do, and then they do it. But they don't realize I'm the one who gave them the idea. That's how Miss A got the orange hair. It's kind of like subliminal messages, only I have almost no control over who hears what. Hoping to work that out this year.

"Better get your room assignment and settle in. Invocation is at five thirty in the Gathering Circle."

The Gathering Circle, or GC, is the main meeting room at Dowling. It's the only room in the building big enough to hold all the Dowling girls. There are some girls who have been here for six years. Even longer, if they're full-fledged witches.

Some Dowling students never leave—they return year after year to teach future witches.

I walk to the welcome desk, manned by two fourth circle witches. That's what I'll be next year if I make it through this one.

"Hi, Hallie," one of the girls says. I don't know her, so I'm surprised she knows who I am. She hands me my ID, which holds a picture taken of me today. I have no clue how they do it, but they always manage to get a picture of us the day we arrive without our knowing. And voilà! It appears on our badge. That kind of thing is hard to get used to.

Just as I'm about to walk away, the other girl sneers at me. "Good luck this year, Hallie. Not that you're going to need it." The last part is said under her breath, but I hear it anyway.

Of course they know who I am.

Everyone knows who I am.

I am the first student at Dowling to have the gift of inheritance since High Priestess Dannabelle Grimm was here in the 1800s. Apparently, that's kind of a big deal. All I really wanted to be was a hedge witch like my great-great-grandmother, mixing herbs and potions to heal and cast spells. But I got a lot more than I bargained for.

I walk away and smile back at the girls, whose faces wear frozen, fake smiles. Miss A said people would be jealous. She was right.

I look at my badge. My room number is 202.

I climb the stairs two at a time, anxious to see the room I'll share with Ivy. During the first year, Seekers are required to room with whomever Dowling assigns you to.

For me, that meant my worst enemy of all time: Kendall Scott. Being able to choose my roommate this year is a big deal. Huge.

I hit the top of the stairs and find the hallway crammed with girls talking, hugging, and snapping fingers. Small bursts of magic appear as girls show off their still-new skills. One girl keeps walking through a wall and back again. Back and forth, back and forth, her friends begging to see her do it "just one more time." It's hard not to watch her, because it's crazy cool. A different girl farther down the hallway has accidentally (I think) frozen a girl's legs in a block of ice. There are probably six or seven girls around the frozen girl, chipping at the ice.

I can't stop smiling. Even though it's a madhouse, it's my madhouse. Home.

"Hallie!" Dru Goode, still a foot shorter than everyone else, pushes her way through the cluster of girls to get to me.

She breaks through, and I smile when I see her. Her perfect white teeth are in direct contrast to her dark skin and black curly hair. It's impossible not to love her. I hug her close, then look behind her.

"Where's Jo?"

Dru shrugs. "I haven't seen her. What room are you in?"

"202," I tell her.

She pushes my shoulder so hard I nearly fall. "Get out! We're in 204! We're neighbors!"

"You're stronger than you look," I tell her, laughing.

I send a silent thank-you to Miss A. I know she's the reason our rooms are next to each other.

I look at the room numbers on the wall and realize I'm standing in front of my door. "Have you gone in your room yet?" I ask Dru.

"Yep," she says. "Same as last year."

I swipe my ID in the door scanner, and the door unlocks. I push it open and—just as Dru said—the rooms are identical to last year's, with one big difference: there's a laptop on each of our desks.

I spin to face Dru. "I didn't know we were getting laptops!"

"Me neither," she says. "But don't get too excited. I hear we have super-limited Internet access."

"Still, we can at least check our e-mail." I look at Dru. "Can't we?"

Dru nods. "Miss A said we could. But no Facebook."

Good. As long as we have e-mail, I'm golden.

My trunk sits in front of one of the beds. Ivy's trunk is already here too. "Your trunk make it here okay?"

Dru nods. "I don't even care how it happens. I'm just glad I didn't have to haul it upstairs. Those trunks are heavy!"

There are definitely perks to being a witch.

"I wish I'd brought my glow-in-the-dark pj's from home. They've got a picture of my family on them," I say.

"Your pj's?" Dru asks, a sneaky smile on her face. "At home? Two hundred long miles from here?"

"Dru, are you sure you know what you're doing?"

She puts her fists on her hips. "I'll pretend you didn't just say that."

I throw my hands up in apology. "You're right. What was I thinking?" Dru's gift of conjuration has come in handy before. Like when she produced a hair straightener before the dance at Riley Academy, where I met Cody.

Cody Ray. The "it" guy at Dowling's brother school, Riley Academy. We met at last year's social, and no matter how hard I tried to discourage him, he was glued to me all night long. I've seen girls ignore their friends because of boys, and I swore I'd never be one of them. Besides, life at Dowling was complicated enough. The last thing

I needed was a distraction. But that's exactly what I got.

Dru closes her eyes and puts her fingers in snapping position. She peeks out at me. "Where do you keep your pj's at home?"

"My dresser. Bottom drawer."

She closes her eyes again and takes a deep breath. She whispers words I can't hear, and tiny, colorful sparks dance off her fingertips.

I look at my desk, then high-five Dru.

Sitting there beside my laptop are the pj's I'd left behind.

Real life. Real you.

Don't miss
any of these
terrific
Aladdin M!X
books.

Enjoy these sweet treats from Aladdin.